The Quickest Chase

Walk of Faith

Table of Contents

CHAPTER ONE 1

CHAPTER TWO.. 5

CHAPTER THREE.. 20

CHAPTER FOUR... 42

CHAPTER FIVE... 53

CHAPTER SIX 72

CHAPTER SEVEN 93

CHAPTER ONE

Seditionist HQ - Los Angeles

At 12:15pm Hank was on his fourth cup of coffee and dying slowly in a tedious meeting with the auditors, but he perked up and hastily excused himself when he saw Floyd's call coming in.

"Greetings, this is Hank Bancroft, how may I assist you today?" he asked formally.

"Dad? It's me."

"I'm sorry, who is this? Do I know you?"

Groan . "You suck so bad, it's not even funny."

Floyd really *was* mad enough to scold his dad, but Hank grinned. He knew what was coming next. "Oh? And why is that, exactly?"

"Because I've been a mess all morning thinking you weren't going to let me come home until I'm old enough to retire. Why didn't you tell me? You're so mean."

"Wanted to surprise you."

Floyd grumbled. "Well, surprise, now you get to pay for dry cleaning Uncle Dav's suit because it has my snot and tears all over it. I made such a fool of myself in front of everybody."

"You're welcome, Floyd."

Hank was still grinning, although he felt bad for being so amused by the poor kid's reaction…but he couldn't help it. At least, not until there was an ugly sniffling noise through the phone; evidently said snot had not yet retreated and Hank suddenly felt a huge pang of guilt.

"So, does that mean you hate me again?"

"No. But I really wanted to like it here, and make you proud and…I'm sorry, dad. I'm almost 16 and acting like such a baby."

"No, don't say that. Missing your family is nothing to be ashamed of at any age. I *am* proud of you, Floyd, because you're a good person. Brave, kind, and smart. Don't ever forget that."

"I don't feel brave right now."

"Well, I have a feeling you'll get over it quickly. See you in about three hours. We'll have an early dinner at home and then you're going straight to bed, no complaining. Home school starts at 8am sharp."

"Yes, sir." Floyd actually sounded really happy about that, and Hank was indescribably pleased at the thought of having his boys back together again.

"I have to go back into my meeting now. Be good for Dav."

"I will, I promise. Thanks for letting me go home, dad. Love you."

Thanks for wanting to come home. "Love you too, son. Can't wait to see you."

Hank swallowed the lump in his throat, and went back to his meeting with a glowing heart.

————-

Floyd loved his Uncle Dav, but he wasn't normally the affectionate type. That's why Daven was astonished and rather honored when Floyd scrambled into the car and straight to his side, wrapping his arms around his "uncle."

"Thank you so much for coming to get me. I'm so happy to go home. Can we get some food? I haven't eaten lunch."

Of course food would be the very first thing on his mind. Dav put an arm around Floyd's shoulders and tried to accustom himself to the boy's lanky body pressed up against his own.

"Your dad said no fast food, so we'll go to a restaurant. I know you want to get home as fast as possible, but-"

"No, it's fine. Thank you."

It only took fifteen minutes to get the resort where Dav knew of a restaurant with a private dining room, but Floyd had laid down and was now sound asleep with his head on Daven's leg when they pulled up. He nodded to Lucas as the man looked back at him with a *what should we do?* expression.

"Let's just head home," Dav whispered. "He's out cold."

Lucas gently pulled the big SUV back out and onto the freeway. Daven covered Floyd up with Hank's blanket, and three hours later the teenager woke up a little disoriented and starving, but ecstatic to find himself in his own driveway. He ran inside to find Theo waiting in the living room with Shannon and Starsky and Hutch, who, gleeful upon spotting Floyd, all promptly rolled over to demand belly rubs from their favorite human.

CHAPTER TWO

The Thunderbird pulled up to the garage just as Floyd had finished greeting the dogs and Theo, and Maurice opened the door to let the contingent in the house. Hank's eyes were bleary and bloodshot as he spoke into his cell phone and held up a finger to shush his sons as they watched him come in and set everything down.

"Thanks, Rupe. I'm sure you're right. Keep me posted." He hung up, then turned to his sons. "Hey kiddos, sorry to keep you waiting. Welcome back, Floyd."

Floyd stayed by the dining room table, suddenly feeling overly anxious. He rarely, if ever, saw his dad in such a state of messy fatigue, and all of his anxiety buttons were instantly pushed.

"Yeah, dad. I'm here."

"I can see that," Hank replied wryly as he ran his fingers through his hair and put his keys on the side table. "Actually, I'm so tired that I'm seeing two of you and two of Theo here right now. And possibly three Shannons, unless you brought home a couple more goldens."

Theo shifted on his feet, as uncomfortable about Hank's appearance as his brother was. "Not today. Are you alright, dad? You were supposed to be home hours ago."

"Yeah, you know how it goes. Floyd, wait for me in my study while I change, okay? I'll be right there."

Floyd's stomach twisted into knots at that; the study had been the location of too many deeply unpleasant conversations and very few happy ones. Hank was no less perceptive when tired than he was wide awake, and he caught the aggrieved look on his oldest's face instantly. Before he could say anything, Daven came in the door with Shannon's leash in hand.

"Thanks for watching over her, Theo," he said warmly as he bustled in, failing as usual to stop the door from slamming behind him before Maurice could catch it. Theo let go of the collar and Shannon ran to Dav with all the exaggerated exuberance of a dog who hadn't seen her favorite human in 36 hours. He bent down to hug her, then looked around the room and seemed to realize he had interrupted something not so pleasant. He hastily latched the leash onto her harness and stood back up.

"Did you *just* get home, Hank?" he asked in surprise.

"Yeah. Don't ask. Thanks for going to get Floyd."

There were a hundred things Daven wanted to say about the fact that Hank hadn't slept for over a day, but he would never do so in front of an audience. Perhaps not even to Hank alone.

"No problem. See you tomorrow."

"I'll be in late. Around 10. I'm going to need to meet with you and Rupe right away."

"Of course. Talk to you then."

He left, and Floyd turned to look pleadingly at his dad, who simply turned and walked up the stairs without another word. Floyd had no choice but to go to the study and wait in silence, writhing as he worried and fretted about what his dad was going to do and say about his failure to succeed at boarding school.

Soon enough the door opened, and Hank entered the room in jeans and a Henley. He stopped to hug Floyd briefly, then stood behind his desk, all business. "I hate to pee on your parade, but we have one piece of unfinished business to attend to. Let's get it over with so we can move on."

"You mean...my license?"

Hank extended the piece of pink paper to his son. "Yes. Shred it without argument."

Floyd reached across the desk and took the precious paper, swallowing his despair as he did so. Fighting with his dad within five minutes of being home would be incredibly reckless, and if this was the price he had to pay for being free of the boarding school, then so be it.

Hank had been steeling himself for a big fight, but he was pleasantly surprised with how quickly Floyd complied without any fuss. The boy simply turned and went to the shredder, flipped it on, then hesitated slightly before feeding it in with a visible sigh of resignation. Afterwards he just stood there, staring glumly at the still-grinding teeth.

"Turn it off," Hank said finally, once he couldn't stand the noise anymore.

Floyd switched it off and walked back to stand in front of his dad's desk, looking like his dog had just gotten run over by a car. "Dad, I'm sorry for all this. For fucking up. For being a failure. For everything."

Hank smiled a little. He never minded when his sons swore in private, and in fact was secretly amused by it. In public was another matter, of course...not that they had ever dared to do such a thing.

"Floyd, you're talking to a man who got kicked out of the Boy Scouts, two boarding schools, *and* college. Do you really think I'm judging you right now for merely *choosing* to leave a place that made you so unhappy?"

That brought a smirk out of the teen, and Hank knew then that everything was going to be okay.

"No, I guess not."

"What was it that made you so unhappy? I'm just curious. You don't have to answer, but I don't believe that you were really missing me and Theo that much."

Floyd nervously twisted his hands into the hem of his polo shirt. "I *did* miss you guys."

"Never mind, then. Tell me if and when you want to talk about it. Listen, I'm shot. I got to go to bed. You and Theo can order in whatever you want for dinner."

"Did you and Uncle Dav really meet with Harmon in San Diego?" Floyd asked tonelessly.

Hank felt his heart race for a moment. "Were you watching the news again?"

Floyd nodded. "This morning. It wasn't banned at school. Everyone watches it. I even know that Avery almost got a ticket but you talked the police officer out of it."

Hank sighed. "That's not what...okay, you're back to *not* watching it again. You know something is said about me almost every day that's going to upset you, and most of it is either bullshit or blown out of proportion."

"Not all of it." Floyd remained stone-faced as his dad crossed from behind the desk and stood less than a foot away from him.

"Son, I'm really glad you're back, and I'd like to keep it that way." Hank put his hands on his son's shoulders and squeezed reassuringly. "Whatever I tell you, or don't tell you, is for your own good. If you need to know, you'll know. We've talked about this a hundred times."

Floyd was too stricken to reply right away and Hank hardened his heart against the deep hurt he knew he had just inflicted. But he had to protect his son at any cost.

"Go figure out what you guys want to order for dinner. You know where the credit card is. Don't watch the news without my permission, ever. That's an order. I'm going to bed."

Floyd stood his ground. "Don't trust that asshole, dad."

Hank replied quietly, "I don't, and he knows it. Hell, everyone knows it, and the feeling is mutual. If it makes you feel better, Uncle Dav was really happy with how the meeting went, and he told me I did great. If the most critical and pessimistic man in the world said that, then you *know* everything's good. Okay?"

That was supposed to make Floyd feel better, but Hank saw him tense up even more. Shit.

"I can't relax if I don't know what's going on."

"You don't need to know, Floyd. You're fifteen years old. Enjoy your childhood while you can and leave the rest of this shit to me. I need to go to bed, seriously. I'm dying here. Come on."

Floyd turned and opened the door and followed his dad glumly out to the kitchen. "I'm turning 16 on Monday."

"Yes, I know. That's two years from 18, when you can do whatever you want. Until then, you mind what I tell you."

"Yes, sir. Our phones are definitely being tapped, by the way. I keep hearing that click."

"Shit. Okay. I'll have the line disconnected." He turned around and embraced Floyd in another tight hug. "After dinner you go straight to bed and lights out. I'll wake you up at seven for breakfast and don't want any fussing. This weekend we're going to go look at the new house and then start moving in next weekend. You excited?"

Floyd grinned. "Yeah. I can't wait to see it!"

"Good. Do me a favor, after you order food go downstairs and find Avery. Let him know about the phone and what you heard. I'll talk to him tomorrow about it. Goodnight, Floyd."

"Goodnight, dad. It's really good to be home."

Floyd watched his dad disappear up the steps, and realized he wasn't really sure about that last part. Then he snuck into the library and parked himself in front of the little television that was haphazardly shoved into a corner, and turned the channel to the 5pm local news. It had already long started and they were past the headlines and into sports already. Damn. He changed it to CNN and sat down on the floor next to the couch to watch.

Half an hour later he nearly jumped out of his skin when the door to the library door opened with a creak, and he dropped the remote in his haste to change the channel. Thankfully it was just Avery.

"Hi," the man said quickly as he shut the door behind him. "Something you need to tell me?"

Floyd clicked off the TV and quickly scrambled up and went over to a bookshelf as if he had been browsing for something to read this entire time.

"I'm not sure what you mean," he replied nervously, then gave up the book charade and started to head for the door. "I need to go order dinner for me and Theo. Want anything?"

Avery stayed where he was, effectively blocking Floyd's exit. "You were supposed to tell me about the phones being tapped after you ordered dinner, both of which you didn't do. Then I find you in here watching TV against your dad's orders."

"Um. Are you...are you going to tell him?"

"*Out.*"

"Yes, sir," Floyd replied anxiously as he darted past his father's guard and hurried into the kitchen. Theo was in there, too, making a huge portion of macaroni and cheese, and he turned to glare at his brother.

"Where the hell have you been? I made us dinner since you never ordered it."

"What? Why didn't you ask Chef to make something?"

"Because it would take forever. Where have you been?"

Floyd shrugged. "Reading. Did you know dad met with Harmon?"

Theo stopped stirring the pot for a moment, then renewed the activity with vigor. "Yeah. I was kind of there. In San Diego, I mean. Not at the meeting."

"What...what the fuck, Theo? Why? You knew about this, too?" Floyd complained bitterly.

"Not like a had a choice. Dad told me not to talk about it. Hand me a plate."

"Fuck that. You tell me when these things happen, okay Theody?"

Now Avery's soft voice again, from almost over his shoulder. "Floyd, step outside with me for a moment."

Floyd didn't want to, but he knew better than to disobey any guard. If the statement had been phrased as a question he could stall, perhaps, but this wasn't a question. So he went, and Avery slid the door shut behind them. He looked livid, but his tone was perfectly calm and diplomatic.

"When Hank asks me tomorrow if you complied with his orders tonight, what do you want me to say?"

"I...I want you to say yes, of course."

"Good. Then go to bed, and leave Theo alone about Harmon. He wasn't lying, he can't talk about it. If you get on his case about it again, I'm going to have a word with your dad about what you were doing in his library tonight without permission. Understood?" Avery crossed his arms. "Your father expects so much better of you, Floyd. We all do."

"Yes, sir, I'm sorry," Floyd whispered shakily, thoroughly rattled. His breath hitched for a moment, and his eyes burned fiercely at the stinging rebuke. Avery had never spoken to him so harshly before. He sounded just like his dad. It hurt.

"Are you hungry?"

"Yes. I haven't eaten since breakfast."

"Then take a plate with you upstairs. Go. Lights out in thirty minutes. I'll be checking to make sure you obey."

Floyd nodded and swallowed hard. "Thank you. I'm sorry."

Avery patted him reassuring on the shoulder, then went back downstairs to his office, where he mentally prepared himself for losing his job if Hank found out he had interfered in a family matter. He knew Floyd would never throw him under the bus, but the fact that he had gone against Hank's wishes unsettled him thoroughly. So did the realization that he would willingly do it again if it meant saving the teenager from his dad's wrath, and vice versa.

That same evening

"Hey Dav. Listen, you're going to hear tomorrow that the audit didn't go well today. I just wanted to give you a heads up and ask you something."

Daven paused stirring his tea. "What do you mean, Rupe? What happened?"

"The strangest thing came up when they were reviewing our financials. Six different cash payouts were made for 'photographic services' last week. Do you know what that might be?"

"*Photographic services?* No idea. Did you ask Hank?"

"Yeah, I was talking to him when he got home. He thinks they might have been miscategorized, but it looks exactly like he paid off those damned photographers after all. The auditors red-flagged it to Stewart without giving us any time to investigate. We've got to figure it out before he gets summoned again."

"Well, I'm sure there's some back-up somewhere. The accounts payable rep who made the payments should be able to explain."

Rupert sighed. "That's just the thing that set off the alarm. We can't tell who did it. Our system allows anonymous transactions with Hank's written authorization, and he's used it a few times for highly confidential reasons. Like severance payouts and things, all above board. But not this time. It has to be a mistake because he says he didn't authorize a damned thing. Normally these transactions are hidden, but somehow they showed up anyway. If he can't convince Stewart this wasn't his doing, we're all in deep shit."

Daven abandoned his tea in the kitchen and went to sit down on the couch. "I don't think it was a mistake, but rest assured that Stewart knows Hank's smart enough not to lead a trail back to him by actually coding the transactions correctly and allowing them to be seen."

Rupe's heart nearly stopped at that. "What are you implying, exactly?"

"That someone is either embezzling from us and just happened to use a code that looks suspicious...or more likely, they're purposely trying to get Hank in trouble. I know you and Hank think everyone on the staff is perfectly loyal and upright, but I don't. Harmon wasn't telling the truth when he said he doesn't employ any double agents."

"You don't know that for sure."

"Neither do you."

Rupe mused over that for a few moments. "Jesus Christ. Let's hope you're wrong. But then again, if you are...never mind. Who is our most trustworthy person in accounts payable? I want only one single person to have access to making anonymous payments, so we can stop this in its tracks."

Daven thought about it for a moment; it was a toss-up between three men who had been on staff the longest.

"Probably Yannick. He's been with us for five years, never any complaints or trouble. He's a bit of an odd one, though, I think we should question the entire accounting staff to find out who did this. There's 24 of them, it will take time to do a polygraph on everyone."

"Time we don't *have* , Dav. Hank can only delay Stewart for so long."

"Well, we can't just choose a select few. It's either all of them, or none at all."

Shit. "Okay, let's do it this way. If we're going to choose one person to have access in the future, we should poly him alone to make sure he's above board. That way we don't have to explain or accuse anyone right off the bat. You want to pick Yannick, then?"

"Yes."

"Okay. If Hank approves we'll talk to Yannick tomorrow morning, poly him in the afternoon. If you're comfortable with him and can trust him with the access, I'm good with that. Then we'll poly the rest as fast as possible before Stewart can pull out his guillotine again. Hopefully, anyway."

Daven paused for a long, anxious moment before responding. "We have to eliminate the possibility that Hank did make the payments. It's our duty. He will understand."

Rupert groaned. "Right, thanks. Very comforting."

"Do you disagree?"

"Of course not. But I don't want to go there right now. Not after what happened to get us in deep shit last time."

Daven drummed his fingers on his lap. "No. But that's because we went behind his back with our suspicions. This time, we either ask him about it upfront, or we don't discuss it at all. Period. Which do you prefer?"

Rupert groaned again. "I'd prefer to walk a mile over hot coals than make that decision."

"Then I'll make the decision," Daven answered firmly. "You and I don't discuss it. He didn't do it, anyway, so there's no point."

"Are you absolutely positive about that?" Rupert asked after a long pause, almost timidly.

"No. But I'm willing to let it go and focus entirely on other possibilities. Are you?"

There was a long silence on the other end of the line.

"Rupert? Are you still there?"

"Ahem. Yeah. I'm sure he didn't do it. You're right, he's way too smart to let it be found. He would have used his own personal money, anyway. End of discussion."

Daven grunted. "Exactly. That settles that. See you tomorrow."

"Wait," Rupe interjected quickly. "No. We *have* to ask him, Dav. He knows that. If we don't, he'll think we are discussing it separately and we'll have Christmas Day all over again. I'll do it."

"No, it's my responsibility. I'll do it."

"Okay. I'll pray for you."

"No need. He's not going to hurt me."

"I was joking, Dav," Rupe sighed.

"Oh. Well, the meeting is at ten o'clock so try not to worry about it until then."

"Right. I'm sure I'll forget all about it."

"Good. See you tomorrow."

They ended the call, and Dav calmly went back to his tea, which to his dismay had become bitter and cold while waiting for his attention.

CHAPTER THREE

Saturday, January 29

Ten days after

Ventura Harbor, California

"Dav, don't unravel it. Just toss it way up. Got to go pretty hard, like-"

The coiled rope splashed into the water of the marina as Daven botched the throw to Hank, who had been reaching for it from the stern of his surprisingly modest 45-foot sailboat.

"You throw like a girl!" Hank complained with a grin as he wiped away the splashes of seawater from his face.

"Sorry. It was heavier than I expected."

"I got it, dad," Theo yelled as he dodged around his "uncle" and retrieved the line, throwing it smoothly into his dad's hands while clambering aboard at the same time. Floyd was busy at the helm, fighting against the tide to keep the boat in the slip so it didn't leave anyone behind.

"Uncle Dav," he called over the gratingly harsh noise of the new engine. "You coming?"

"Do I have a choice?" Dav grumbled as he waited for the bow to come closer before taking the huge step up from the dock. He made it without any further mishaps, to everyone's relief.

As Floyd navigated them into the open waters of the large marina, Hank walked along the decks and methodically pulled the fenders up over the sides.

"Boys, start untying the sails. Dav, come sit with me at the helm."

It wasn't often that Daven joined Hank and his sons on sailing adventures, and his clumsiness and general disinterest in the activity was primarily why. Not to mention his tendency to become seasick long before they could make it out of the smooth harbor.

"Sorry, Hank," he said sheepishly as he sat down next to his boss.

"No problem. Want something to drink?"

"Ginger ale, please."

Hank glanced aside at Maurice. "Ginger ale for Dav and the boys. Root beer for me. See if we have any Cheez-its." The man nodded and disappeared underneath the hatch to join the rest of the servants and the two guards, who always stayed below on these trips to allow the family some much-needed privacy. Once the drinks and food had arrived, Hank would close the hatch and it would almost feel like they were alone in the world again. Almost.

"I can't believe it's this warm and nearly February," he mused conversationally. "Got to love California. We'd be freezing our asses off in Kansas right about now."

"Mmmmm," Dav replied noncommittally, zipping up his windbreaker and looking slightly green. "Maybe I should get on a plane, then, since I prefer hypothermia over dry heaves."

Hank barked out a laugh, and his two boys turned around to look at him and grinned.

There was silence for about ten minutes, except for Hank's necessary commands to the boys in regards to the sails. He was never a tyrant at sea and was a surprisingly easygoing and humorous captain. Floyd and Theo loved these trips because they almost felt like a normal family again, and they didn't have to walk on eggshells around their dad for a few hours. Their mom had loved sailing, and the boat was named after her. Accordingly, Hank loved it, too, and he was at his most relaxed when behind the helm. For the Bancrofts, this was as normal as life would ever get.

As the boat nudged its bow into the deeper waters of the Pacific, Floyd pulled up the mainsail hand over hand while Theo worked on the mizzen. Once they were officially sailing, Hank cut the engine and adjusted his ears to the startling quiet while Maurice emerged with the drinks and snacks. While he wasn't really needed out here just to bring a few trays up and down, Hank always brought him along because he loved sailing.

"You take your seasickness stuff?" he asked with a straight face, as he always did.

Maurice grimaced. "No, sir. Going to be throwing up all over your beautiful boat today, I'm afraid."

"Try to keep it to a bare minimum this time."

"Yes, sir."

"Thank you."

Maurice disappeared below while Hank chuckled to himself. The man had an iron stomach and would possibly be the last person in the world to get seasick. But Hank always poked fun at him anyway, which was particularly fun to do in front of Daven, who was now a much darker shade of green.

"Hey, Dav. Take the wheel." That would give him something to do to keep his mind off his stomach. Hank picked up the two cans of ginger ale and went forward to hand them to the boys. They all sat down on the forward hatch and drank in silence.

"Dad," Floyd said eventually. "Can we just stay out here forever?"

"No. The dogs would miss you too much. How about all day, instead?"

"Sure. But don't you have work to do?"

"Nope. You guys want to take a turn at the wheel?"

"I do!" Theo interjected excitedly. With a strong breeze like this, Hank usually never let the boys take over the steering. But it was blowing straight, and the waves were minimal. Even Daven was having no trouble keeping her on course.

"Okay. Go take over from Uncle Dav."

Theo departed excitedly, and Hank was left sitting alongside his oldest son. They hadn't spoken much in the past week and a half, but when they had, Floyd had been pleasant and compliant, causing no trouble at all. It had been a remarkably peaceful ten days since he returned from boarding school.

"Hey. How are you doing?" Hank asked eventually.

"Good, thanks. You?"

"You seem a bit down. Just...you know, you can talk to me. I'm here. Anytime."

"Thank you."

Well, so much for that. Floyd was staring out at the horizon, and his mind was anywhere but on this boat. Hank patted him on the shoulder and stood up.

"Wait, dad..."

Hank staggered against a wave that pitched the boat as he turned back, and the momentum forced him neatly back down onto the spot where he had just been sitting.

"Oomph. Yeah?"

Floyd swallowed hard. "There is actually something that I need to tell you."

Oh god. Guilt detected. Hank knew his kids, and that's undoubtedly what Floyd's flat tone indicated. Well...so much for a relaxing day.

"What did you do?" he asked tersely.

Floyd shot him a hurt look. "Nothing!"

"Sorry. What's on your mind, I meant to ask?"

"Well, it's just that...that I'm sixteen years old now, and it doesn't make sense anymore for me not to know what's going on around me. I really don't like being in the dark. I was wondering if you would possibly reconsider your rule about not letting me watch the news."

Hank shuddered, then gulped down the last of his root beer. "Yes."

"Dad, please, I just want...wait. What?" Floyd stared at his father in wonder and surprise, eyebrows furrowed.

"I said yes, I'll reconsider, because you asked so nicely and told me what was bothering you without starting a fight. But I want to ask you something first, and I expect an honest answer. Have you been watching it without my permission?"

Floyd felt a lump in his throat. "Just once, the day I got home from Palm Springs. You went to bed so early and left the library unlocked...but I haven't done it again. Haven't even touched the TV at all, because I felt so bad about it, I swear. I'm sorry, dad."

Hank rested an arm lightly around his son's tense shoulders. "Yeah, I knew about that. Avery spilled the beans."

"He did?" Floyd responded in horror. "And you didn't even you didn't get mad?"

"Oh yeah, I was mad. Still am, but you haven't watched it since then, so I'll get over it. In the future we'll watch it together, and you're not to watch it without me, ever. Agreed?"

Floyd nodded, still in shock. "Why...why didn't you say anything about it?"

"Because Avery asked me not to. You feel like doing some fishing?"

Floyd stared askance at his dad for the third time in as many minutes. "Dad...I...are you feeling alright?"

Hank was desperate to tell him the truth. To lay down his burdens and tell *anyone* , really, that *no* ...he wasn't alright. Not by a longshot. That Stewart's total silence on the audit findings had instilled a sense of doom on him, keeping him awake for four nights straight. That he hated himself for allying with Harmon. That he disliked his own constituents and was secretly planning to destroy their ballot measures at all costs. That he knew Dav and Rupert quietly suspected that he paid the photographers off, despite his insistence that he didn't and their easy acceptance of his denial.

That doing the right thing had never felt so wrong, and that he knew his career would end sooner than planned, no matter what he did to prevent it.

Worst of all...that something dark within his soul *wanted* this. *Wanted* his name to live in infamy, along with his face from that famous photograph. *Wanted* to be a martyr for his party.

He didn't know why he couldn't fight off those thoughts anymore.

"Yeah, Floyd, I'm good. You know how much I love being out on the ocean. Makes me feel like myself again."

"But that's the thing. You're not *yourself* at all, dad. You're freaking me out."

"Hmmm. And here I was thinking you'd be relieved that I'm trying really hard to go easier on you and Theo. If you prefer, I can just take off my belt right here and-"

"No, no!" Floyd laughed nervously. "I *am* relieved. Please don't. Sorry I asked."

"I won't," Hank replied seriously. "The truth is that apparently I'm a big old softy when my boys are behaving. Who would have thought?"

The sarcasm wasn't quite lost on Floyd, but it didn't exactly hit its target, either.

"Oh. Okay. Dad?"

"What?"

"Do you think you'll be re-elected in November?"

Hank felt his blood pressure rise sharply at the query, but he kept his tone level. "I don't know."

"But we have enough money that it doesn't matter if you aren't, right?"

"Yes. We'll be fine, Floyd."

Hank withdrew his arm and shoved his hands into the pockets of his sweatshirt. He wanted to tell his son he wasn't going to run again and they'd all be free of this life, one way or another. And that was assuming he even made it to November without being thrown out of office.

"Look. A lot can happen between now and then. A lot *will* happen, and that's the only thing I can guarantee. Let's just focus on the present. Tonight we start packing for the new house, and in three weeks we move in. I want you to keep your attention on that, okay? And on school, obviously. Mrs. Aster is brutal with the homework, so you have a lot on your plate already without worrying about something that's ten months away."

Floyd nodded. "Okay, dad. I just worry, that's all."

"I know. Me too. Let's try to relax today. Want to fish for a little bit?"

"Sure."

Floyd got up and went aft while Hank stayed on the hatch, his thoughts shifting back to packing up the house, and once again wondering if he really should have hired movers instead of enlisting his servants for the task of filling up the pallet of boxes that had just arrived this morning. It wasn't exactly in their job description (not that they had one), but he hated beyond reason the thought of having strangers in the house. He knew he was being absurd by worrying about everyone thinking he was trying to be cheap by using "free" labor.

He went back to the cockpit to commend Theo's steering job, then said to Floyd as he was readying the poles, "Make sure they're secured this time."

Theo burst out laughing, then abruptly stopped himself as his dad threw a sharp look at him. Floyd had lost Hank's favorite pole overboard five trips ago, which the poor kid was apparently never going to hear the end of.

"I will, dad," Floyd replied with a sigh, his hopes of being forgiven dashed once again.

Hank suddenly remembered his vow not to be a asshole at sea, so he grinned, ruffled Theo's hair playfully, and went down into his cabin to lay down. He ended up dozing off for the better part of an hour. When he re-emerged into the sunlight, Floyd and Theo had given up fishing and were sitting way up on the bowsprit, waiting patiently for dolphins to appear alongside.

Daven moved aside to make room for Hank to take the helm and murmured very quietly, "I just had quite an enlightening conversation with Floyd. He's convinced Harmon is going to kill us both."

Hank groaned. "Oh geez. He's...I'm sorry, Dav."

"It's no problem. I tried to change the subject several times, but he's persistent. Have you changed your mind about meeting with him again?"

"No. Speaking of Harmon, though, I've got something bothering me and would really appreciate your perspective on it."

"Of course."

"I've been trying not to say anything for a while, because I'm not completely sure how I feel about the whole thing and didn't want to start any fights before I worked it out within my head. But I've got to be honest, Dav. We are completely wrong about supporting public flogging, and the tightening of restrictions on Bonded Retainers."

Dav nodded. "I know you think that, Hank. We all do. There's no other reason for you to delay approving the public statement for so long."

"What does Rupert say about it all?"

"He's frustrated, of course. Wants to get the thing out."

Hank took a deep breath and steeled himself. "No, I don't mean that. I mean…how does he feel about the measures? Does he support them?"

Daven took a long draw of his grape soda. "It's not for me to say, Hank. You should ask him."

"I'm asking you."

"Well, I'm not telling you, because I'm not inside his mind."

Hank noted a sudden shift in the wind, as did they boys. They jumped up to loosen the sails in order for a course change, and once it was done they started to come aft. Hank caught Floyd's eye and shook his head slightly, and noted with pride the way his son immediately understood the meaning. Floyd subtly redirected his brother around to sit on the bow again, and Hank picked up the conversation from where they had left off before he could lose his nerve.

"What would you say if I said we're going to oppose them both and ally with Harmon in our messaging?"

"We've run with Harmon's messaging before, Hank, and vice versa. So I would say, fine, let's do it. What is it about *this* particular subject that's upsetting you so much?"

"Oh, nothing. Just the little fact that our constituents are total assholes and will run me out of office for betraying them and their vengeful ideals. That's all, no big deal."

Daven nodded. "Probably."

"Probably? Thanks for making me feel better, Dav!" Hank replied in disgust.

"You didn't hire me to make you feel better. My job is to find out the truth to help guide your decisions. Opposing those measures is going to cost you. All of us, actually."

"Great. That's even more comforting. Thanks."

Maurice suddenly slid open the hatch to announce lunch was ready, and Hank snapped harshly at him, "Wait until I tell you *we're* ready!"

Daven stood up and set down his bottle. "I need to use the restroom, Hank."

"The head."

"What?"

Sigh . "The toilet on a boat is called...you know what, never mind."

"Okay. Be right back."

That was the end of the conversation for now; Hank knew. Daven had ways of defusing him that he couldn't fight back against, and suddenly having to make an exit for personal needs was one of them. He would most likely stay awhile for a while to let Hank's temper cool. Damn it.

Hank pulled out his phone, then remembered he had no signal out here. But he could still read emails that had already come in, and scrolled down to the latest from Harmon.

Hank, just learned of some new intel regarding measures that will be on the April ballot. I know it's far away, but we should talk. No doubt we'll disagree on all except one, which I think you should be made aware of sooner or later as it affects both of our sons directly. I think you catch my meaning. If you're up for dinner again, let me know. - Harmon

Once again, Hank felt a sweet taste of victory rush through his heart. That could only mean one thing; Harmon had introduced him to Colton Gamble, and now Hank's measure regarding prohibiting photographers from selling photos of minors had passed through the house. There was no reason for any of their constituents to downvote it. Soon Theo and Floyd would be free of the harassment that had made all of their lives so miserable.

————-

February 9

FBI Headquarters - Philadelphia

Salome Danby was often unhappy, good fortune often missing out of her life, but this level of unhappiness was new and untested. She didn't know why she cared so much about Hank Bancroft, or why Stewart felt the same, or even why the president himself tried so hard to keep the man in line and in office. But they all did care about him, for whatever reason, which made the most recent report even more disappointing than the last.

"Salome, may I come in?"

Stewart was standing at the office door, realizing his boss hadn't even seen him approaching because she was so engrossed in the stack of papers in front of her.

"Sure. You may not want to, though, after what I'm about to show you."

"Oh god. What did Hank do now?" He sat down and took a mint from the candy bowl as Salome handed him a printed copy of an email that she had received the day before.

"Senator Gamble?" Stewart exclaimed immediately.

"Yes. Read it."

--

To: Office of Ethics and Integrity

Salome Danby, Director

Ms. Danby, it is my obligation to report to you that yesterday, Feb 8, Hank Bancroft called me from his cell phone to offer cash for pushing his recent measure through the House for the April 1 ballot. I declined, of course. Under the Whistleblower Act I exercise my right to decline to answer any further questions regarding this matter unless required by a lawful process.

Regards,

Colton Gamble

"There is no way Hank did that," Stewart scoffed immediately, handing the paper back to Salome in disgust. "Absolutely no way. He's smarter than that, not to mention more ethical. This is bullshit."

"Colton has no reason to lie. None," Salome refuted sternly.

"Except that he used to work for Harmon! That gives him all the reason in the world."

"Harmon fired him from his dream job, Stewart. They hate each other."

Stewart sat back in his chair. "Oh…that's right."

"Colton was really tight with Colbert, and I remember that the incident caused friction between him and Harmon. Add it to Hank's file. We can't ask him about it directly unless there is evidence, so we'll check his phone records next cycle. Have you questioned him about the photography payments yet?"

"No. We've contacted four of the six photographers involved in that incident, and none have had anything to say about it. They're either lying, or they weren't paid and it really was a glitch in the financials."

"Urbanes lying? To the FBI?" Salome asked in mock incredulity. "Who would imagine such a thing. Keep trying to contact the other two. There's no rush. We just have to do this right."

"I think it would be very strange of them to lie in order to protect an Seditionist."

"Not if they were promised future payments for complying. Or for their silence."

"Right. We've also discovered that Hank did disconnect his home phone. I'd say he knew we were tapping him, but the family is moving to a new house in two weeks and it could just be a utilities changeover."

Salome smiled a little. "No. He knew, and it's not a crime to unplug a phone. Leave it alone for now. It's not like we were getting anything out of it, anyway."

Stewart nodded. "Hank is much smarter than that. If he really *did* call Senator Gamble yesterday, I guarantee you it won't be in his phone records. He'll have used a secondary phone we aren't auditing so that we can't prove anything without issuing a subpoena for statements."

"Even then we can't prove anything. I couldn't ever have imagined Hank offering money like this before, but now that he's proved he's capable of it with that photographer business, I don't think we can put anything past him."

"No." Stewart was slightly depressed to discover he felt the same way. "I'm still upset we still haven't resolved the mystery behind his calls to a Colorado cell number at the time of Janet's murder, either. Until that's cleared, I guess we should keep all the possibilities on the table."

Salome opened her laptop back up, signaling the imminent end of the meeting. "I'm inclined to believe the senator, Stewart. Off the record, of course. You're free to believe whatever you'd like, but we can't let our opinions influence our investigation."

"No ma'am."

Stewart went back to his desk, and for an hour he grudgingly resisted the urge to pick up the phone and call Hank Bancroft to ask him about it directly.

He desperately wanted Salome to be wrong, but he strongly suspected she wasn't.

After another long struggle with his logic going around in circles, he gave in and picked up the phone.

Seditionist HQ - Los Angeles

Hank didn't want to get out of the car. He was tired and the day hadn't even begun yet. His calendar was already packed with meetings, and he wouldn't even have privacy at lunch thanks to the monthly birthdays party for the office. Normally he enjoyed those occasions immensely, as it took him out of his normal schedule and allowed him to socialize and relax for a little while before tackling the afternoon.

He dug his phone out of his pocket as the phone rang.

"Hey, Dav."

"Rupe and Taylor and I are in the conference room. Do you want us to wait, or shall we reschedule?"

Sigh. "I'm downstairs. Coming. Wait…I have an incoming call from Stewart. Shit. Don't leave, okay? Just wait for me."

He clicked over to the incoming call.

"Hank Bancroft."

"Morning, Hank. I just need a second. Are you alone?"

"Yes I am. How can I help you?"

"Quick question, off the record. Your measure is going to be on the April 1 ballot. Were you aware of that?"

"Not officially. Rumors only. Glad to hear it."

"And Colton Gamble helped you with that?"

Pause. "Yes. All above board and via official channels. Harmon introduced me to him directly. Why do you ask?"

"So…it was *Harmon* who introduced you to him?" That was odd.

"Yes. I thought it was strange, considering their history. But as I said, all above board. Is something wrong?"

Stewart cleared his throat. "No, sorry. The question I called to ask is whether or not there was any, uh, compensation that passed between the two of you for his assistance. Or any offer of compensation. This is not an accusation, Hank, let me be clear."

"Between me and Harmon? Of course not!"

"No, I meant…between you and Senator Gamble."

"I can't believe you're even asking me this," Hank replied, rightfully indignant. "Obviously you have some kind of suspicion, or you wouldn't have called. What's going on?"

Oh shit, Stewart thought frantically. *I never should have called. If Salome finds out about this, my ass is so grass….*

"Just look at it from my point of view. Passing a brand new measure in the House within a week is unheard of. And this Senator isn't known for his quick action on anything. Surely you can understand our concern?"

That relaxed Hank a little, and he backed off on the attitude, although his tone was still sharp. "I do. But if you remember that my measure helps Harmon's son as well, you'll realize who Colton was really in it for. He didn't care about what I want. He just wants to kiss Harmon's ass and try to get back on his good side. *That's* why he lit a fire under it. Any more questions, Stewart? I'm late for a meeting."

"No. Thank you for your time, Hank."

Hank hung up without saying goodbye, and stormed upstairs into the conference room where his team was waiting impatiently. He took a copy of Rupert's draft media statement out of his briefcase and slowly tore it to shreds as he talked.

"Alright, team. I've heard all of your arguments, opinions, and strategies. Thank you for your thoughtful input and valid concerns. I've made my decision. The Seditionists are officially opposing these March 1 measures. There will be no tolerance for public flogging, or indentured servitude for minors under our watch, and that's the end of it. Rupert, get out a pen and paper. We need a new media statement that allies us with the Urbanes."

Rupert reached into his briefcase to comply, then took a deep breath as he uncapped his pen.

"You might finally start a revolt with this one, Hank," he murmured quietly. "At the very least, our constituents will throw you out of office on March 2."

"*Another* revolt, you mean. Let them. You all agreed with me that these measures are wrong, never mind the ones that passed in October thanks to the damned elitists. It's about time we all got the balls to fight back against them." He looked at Taylor apologetically. "What's the female equivalent of that saying?"

"Something about ovaries, maybe? But we don't have a saying, because women are in a perpetual state of fighting back. Don't need balls, because we don't rest. Must be why they're retractable."

Hank closed his eyes briefly. "Yeah, never mind. Sorry I asked. Rupe, stop giggling and start writing."

CHAPTER FOUR

Urbane Headquarters - Denver

"It isn't just for show, Colbert," Harmon repeated for the third time. "Hank is putting his career at risk by aligning with us. He knows this is the right thing. You know what he told me? That he's totally prepared to lose his job over this March 1 vote. Come November, he probably will."

Colbert wasn't convinced by this line of thinking; he knew Hank far too well to resist cataloguing this sudden capitulation as anything but another devious scheme.

"Is that why you talked him into it? To turn his constituents against him?"

Harmon laughed. "Have you ever been able to talk Hank into anything? Because I haven't. He does what he wants, and *only* what he wants. This was *his* decision. Look, I know you hate the guy, but he's not up to anything this time."

"He's always up to something. Always. He was conspiring to get me thrown in jail while having dinner with my family on Thanksgiving Day."

"That was ten years ago. Are you ever going to stop bringing it up on a weekly basis?"

Harmon knew it was a rhetorical question, but he couldn't stop himself from asking anyway for the hundredth time. Colbert would forever be unable to forgive his former compatriot for publicly exposing their own party's private communications in the middle of the Second American Revolution. The immediate backlash over Colbert's unspeakably treacherous plans as leader of the Seditionists forced the rebels to all but disband and morph into multiple factions, and Colbert - along with his entire leadership team - was quickly jailed for the rest of the war by President Durdan for making terroristic plots against the government.

Hank's whistle blowing was the reason the more radical group of Urbanes came into existence in the first place, and it thrilled modern historians that one single clerk with a dislike of attracting attention to himself could cause such a rift in the historical timeline of the nation. And not just once - the infamous candid photo of him at a protest had started the war, after all. It thrilled the historians even more that the same man now led the party he had torn apart at the seams, and social studies textbooks went on for pages about the incidents. They claimed Hank ultimately saved the rebellion singlehandedly by insisting upon more peaceful conflict resolution, which was all part of the reason he was currently so popular amongst the more conservative citizens of the Reunited States. Which, in consequence, was also the reason why his followers had been steadily tightening the noose on criminal behavior since then.

Harmon had considered Hank a hero at the time, but that was before he discovered his own radical leanings. Once he did, he left the Seditionists and worked his way up over two years to take over as leader of the Urbanes. Then he hired Colbert the moment he was out of jail after the government fell, and the rest was history.

"I'm just reminding you, Harmon, in case you've forgotten," Colbert grumbled angrily. "Bancroft was my secretary, trusted by everyone with their lives, and he threw us under the bus faster than you can count to three. I never saw it coming, and you're not seeing it this time, either. He's up to something, and you're going to get-"

Harmon stood up abruptly. "Alright, that's enough. You can't keep letting the past dictate the future. We've cooperated with Hank before, and you barely said a word about it. Why complain now? Are you in support of those measures and haven't told me yet, or what? Explain to me what the problem is."

Colbert blinked a few times and uncrossed his arms. "The problem is that you're trusting Hank Bancroft after he has spent years trying to bring you down. I don't understand it."

"You're wrong. I don't trust him, and think he's a complete dick. You know that without even having to ask. These measures are for the good of the nation, and if he can help us get them passed, then more power to us. We need the support of his constituents."

"Not going to happen. He's going to oppose the measures. He's playing you. Daven and Rupert will never agree to go against the party line."

"They already have," Harmon interrupted quietly as he reached over to his printer and handed the new email from Hank to his irate second-in-command. "I just got a preview of their media statement that's going out in ten minutes. Take a look."

Same time

Seditionists HQ - Los Angeles

"Well, Hank," Rupert said with a sigh as he placed the statement into the fax machine for distribution through the wire service. "It's been nice working with you. I suppose you've chosen new leadership for the party already? You're going to need them in about fifteen minutes."

Hank didn't look up, but smiled a little as he tapped his pen on his desk calendar. March 1 was 18 days away. Perhaps enough time to reason with his constituents, perhaps not...

"Relax, Rupe. We'll have until November to figure that out. Are you absolutely certain that holding off on a press conference is a good strategy? I feel like we should have one today."

"No," replied Daven from his post next to the window, where he was watching hungrily as a large group of people on the street crowded around a food truck. "I'd say no less than 24 hours, but I'm not the PR guy."

"Absolutely not today," Rupert agreed. "Even longer than that. I'd say 48 hours. Until then, say your prayers."

"I already have," Dav answered seriously.

"Stop it." Hank frowned as he set his pen back in the holder and stood up to stretch. "No more gloom and doom. We agreed on a strategy, so we have to willingly and calmly take the consequences. Neither one of you indicated you want to back down so far. Any change to that?"

Rupert and Daven looked at each other, then at Hank, then solemnly shook their heads.

"Right. So. There we have it." He looked at Rupert and nodded once. "Hit the transmit button."

Rupert appeared to count to ten before taking a deep breath and pushing the button, a move which he performed with his usual dramatic flair. Then the three men stood around like statues, rooted to the carpet as the fax machine began its ministrations. Lost in their own thoughts, no one looked at each other as the process was carried on. After several minutes when the transmittal receipt was spitting out and the tension was winding down, Hank finally spoke up.

"Gents. Look at me." When they had both complied, he took a deep breath. "I'm grateful to stand beside you in this moment. I'm proud of you both. Of all of us. We'll get through this, okay? We're doing the right thing. You *know* that."

"Yes, sir," they both said together in matching melancholy tones. *Sir.* Not what Hank wanted to hear at the moment from his two best friends. But he was quickly cheered when Daven's stomach rumbled loudly, breaking the seriousness of the moment.

"Sorry," Dav mumbled, his cheeks flushing red in embarrassment.

"I'm hungry, too," Hank replied as he turned to put his coat on. "Let's go down the block to Blue Daisy. My treat."

"Are you sure it's a good idea for us to appear in public right now?" Daven asked somberly.

"Yes," Hank and Rupe said together, then Hank added, "We have to appear as normal as possible. Business as usual. Disappearing from view after such a controversial statement would be the worst possible course right now. Come on."

The three friends left the room and went downstairs; Hank was too rattled to think of taking a moment for the others to grab their jackets from their offices down the hall. The little group crossed the street in silence, two of the trio clutching themselves against the wind, and all three shaking from the cold and frayed nerves.

Behind them their guards followed closely, peacefully unaware of the shitstorm that was about to slam them all.

The death threats started immediately. Hank's email address somehow became public by late afternoon, as did his cell phone number. The same fate befell Daven and Rupert. All three of them were inundated with messages from irate constituents, and Hank's assistant had quite a task on her hands trying to sort through the mess. She forwarded the few messages of support to his alternate, secret email address, which failed to cheer him even one bit.

But what did cheer him was the knowledge that people still had the lack of sense in this day and age to send their deeply disturbing threats in ways that made them easily identifiable. He had Ellen forward the worst email threats to his contact at the police department, and on the way home he would stop by to play the voicemails for them to hear. Those idiots would be quickly arrested, and hopefully unable to vote come March 1. The people Hank really worried about were the ones who might be serious about doing something, in which case they would keep their identities hidden.

But then again…all this had happened before, and all this would happen again. No one at Seditionists headquarters was fazed by the media and satellite tracks filling up the streets - it could hardly be worse than it was after Hank threatened Harmon last year on live television - but as Hank packed up to leave at 5pm he realized he had forgotten all about the impact this would have on Theo and Floyd. Last year, they had been at their grandfather's house in Wyoming when shit went down, and were blissfully unaware of all that followed.

This time, though…they would know. The house would be swarmed by media, the streets belatedly blocked at both ends by police. He looked at his phone for the first time in hours and saw seven missed calls from Floyd within the last half hour, then two from Theo.

Then one from Brittany only thirty seconds ago.

Shit.

He decided to call Brittany back first from the speakerphone on his desk while he packed his briefcase.

"You guys okay?" he asked quickly. "I'm leaving the office in five minutes."

"Theo's fine. Floyd's having a panic attack from all the mess out front. He thinks something happened to you. Maurice's helping him through it now."

"Let him know I'm okay and will be home soon. I have to go. Are the police there to keep the idiots off my lawn?"

"Yes. You need to talk to him," Brittany insisted, and Hank agreed.

"Hey kiddo."

"Dad! What the...what the..."

Hank tried to keep his voice cheerful. "Oh, the usual...your dad made the news again, but this time it's for a good reason. Everything's okay. I'll explain when I get home. You going to be okay?"

"They've been here for hours! Why didn't you call to let us know you're not dead?"

Hank couldn't very well say he forgot all about the very existence of his boys for five hours, so he dodged the question as best he could. "The guards could have let you know, they're all in contact with each other. Ask them next time. Can you-"

"Next time?!"

"Floyd. I'm coming home now. I have to go. Bye."

He hung up and then turned to find Daven standing in his doorway.

"Hey," Hank said casually as he closed the four latches on his briefcase. "Bit of a shitstorm out there."

"You think?"

Hank blinked in surprise; it wasn't like Dav to be sarcastic. When he did, it was always because he was extremely angry about something…and that was rare.

"Are you riding home with me?" he asked neutrally.

Daven shook his head. "No. Going to be here late."

"Nothing you can do in the next few hours will make this better. Don't argue with me, just get packed and let's go. What's wrong, anyway? You seem upset."

"I am. Floyd called me about a hundred times while I was in the strategy meeting. You really didn't think to let your kids know to expect all this mayhem on their front lawn?"

Hank sighed, wondering how to make this better and realizing he couldn't. "No, I didn't, Dav. I'm sorry. I just talked to Floyd and he's okay now."

"No, he's not. He's having a panic attack. I was standing right here and heard it all."

Hank froze. There was something really off about Daven's attitude that he didn't recognize, and he certainly didn't like the tone. But he wasn't going to start a fight with him about it when he was the one in the wrong.

"Alright. Floyd had a panic attack because his father is an idiot. Stay late if you want, then."

"I will. It's not like I have kids to go home to, after all. Kids that would love to know I'm still alive."

Hank walked over to his coat closet and took his time buttoning the woolen jacket all the way down. He felt his temper flare up a little over the man's untimely eavesdropping, but he fought it back down considering they butted in on each other's calls like that all the time.

"Dav, I said I'm sorry. No, I didn't inform the boys. It was thoughtless and stupid, okay? I'm the worst father of the year for like sixteen years in a row now, you shouldn't be surprised. Can you be done glaring at me now, please?"

Hank turned around to look at Daven to check on that last point, and instead found Avery there staring at him in confusion. Awkward.

Hank cleared his throat. "Uh. I wasn't talking to myself, I swear. Where did Dav go?"

"Went into his office about thirty seconds ago, boss. Are you ready for Vance to pull the car around?"

Sigh. "Yes. Let's go home, Avery."

CHAPTER FIVE

Same evening

Bancroft Household

Hank's anger at his guards arose suddenly on the way home, without him even realizing at first what he was mad about. There was just a sort of vague feeling of discontent swirling around in his brain, then it spread to his chest. By the time Vance had fought through the mess of cars to his driveway, he had figured it out and was thoroughly irate from head to toe. As they went through the front door he ordered Avery into his study even before saying hello to Maurice or going up to check on Floyd.

"Explain this to me, please," he began tersely as he shut the door behind him and circled around his favorite guard. "Floyd had a panic attack this afternoon because nobody bothered to tell him his father is still alive. Not only that, but I just learned both my sons were sent home early from school and nobody bothered to tell me. Are you all not communicating with each other? What's the issue here, exactly?"

"Sir, you won't let us tell the boys anything. Brittany knew Floyd was panicking, and she called me for permission to let them know what was happening."

"And you didn't think to ask me for it?"

"No. We already have explicit instructions that say otherwise, as you've reminded me time and again. And Brittany left you a voicemail about them going home early due to the press arriving at Rupert's house."

Neither explanation soothed Hank's temper. "Alright. My fault again for trusting that common sense will always prevail. Obviously, the boys can know I'm alive if they ask. Daven and Rupert are the only ones who have permission to inform them if I'm not. I also need to know when they go home early from school, and not by voicemail. Is that simple enough for everyone to understand, or do I need to dumb it down even further?"

Avery cocked his head a little and looked at his boss with an expression that subtly indicated he would love to throttle the mighty leader of the Seditionists to tiny little bits.

"Crystal clear, sir," he answered calmly.

"Is there something you want to say?" Hank challenged, not yet aware that he was wildly overreacting to what was really his own guilt over the matter.

"Not until you've calmed down."

"Take a number, it's going to be a long wait. Rewrite the policy and send it to me in one hour."

Hank strode past him and hurried upstairs to Floyd. He dreaded this conversation - confrontation, perhaps - and had a feeling he'd regret not waiting until he had collected his thoughts and was in a more polite mood.

Floyd was half-asleep in Theo's bed, while Theo was sitting next to him on the floor, playing video games on the television.

"No, don't get up," Hank said gently to both of them as he sat next to Floyd's limp body. There was a well-used paper bag on the nightstand.

"Hey, I'm here. You okay?"

"Feel sick," Floyd grumbled without moving. "Headache. What's going on? Are you in trouble again?"

"Not at all. I just released a statement today that didn't go over too well with my constituents."

"Your *whats*?" Theo asked.

"A constituent is a member of my party who is eligible to vote," Hank clarified. "Pause your video game for a second, please."

"How many do you have?" Theo asked curiously as he reached over to switch off the Nintendo.

Hank didn't want to say the real number - just over 120 million - because he thought that would be way too much for the boys to take in.

"About a third of the nation, give or take a little."

Theo's eyes went wide. "And they're all mad at you right now?"

"Not all of them." *Only the vast majority of them.*

Floyd flopped over onto his back and eyed his father suspiciously. His hands were trembling.

"So...you didn't do anything wrong this time?"

"Depends on who you ask. My opinion carries a lot of weight, so when I say or do something unexpected, everyone freaks the fuck out."

"Why was it unexpected?'

"It's just like I always say: we do what we think is right, even if everyone else thinks it's wrong, and then we accept the consequences. That's exactly what I did today, and I would do it again in a heartbeat."

Theo pitched in quietly, "If you did the right thing, what is everyone so mad about?"

Hank smiled a little. "Because they're confused about what the right thing actually is. They'll come around."

Floyd scoffed bitterly. "The other right thing to do would have been to let us know you were okay! You said Uncle Dav would always pick up my phone calls no matter what, remember? I called him like 50 times and he never answered, so I thought...I thought..."

Floyd's eyes were misty again, and Hank now had an enormous lump in his throat.

"Not his fault, don't be mad at him. None of our cell phones were working this afternoon. I was going to call you the minute you guys got out of school, but the day got away with me."

"It always does," Floyd muttered.

"I'm really sorry, kiddo," Hank said sincerely as he pulled the blanket up to Floyd's chin. "You're shaking pretty bad. Need some water?"

"Apple juice, please."

Hank looked at Theo, who immediately made his way to the kitchen.

Once he was gone, Hank leaned down to whisper in his other son's ear. "There's something I have to tell you. It's really important you keep it to yourself, because no one else knows yet, and they won't for a long time. It's absolutely critical that you never repeat it. I mean it. You promise?"

Floyd nodded.

"Not good enough. Say out loud that you promise. Swear it."

He did, somewhat nervously, and Hank took a deep breath.

"I'm not going to run again for office in November. This is my last term as leader of the-"

Floyd sat up and threw his arms around his dad, and thoroughly burst into tears. Hank couldn't help it; he cried a little too at the happiness the news gave his son.

"Dad! That's like...that's the *last* thing I expected you to tell me today."

"I mean it when I say you can't tell a soul. Not even Theo. If you do, I swear that I'll-"

"I won't," Floyd insisted urgently, between sniffles. "I *won't*, I promise. Did you get fired?"

"Ha. Who would fire me? I'm the one in charge. Lay back down and relax. You going to be alright?"

Floyd grinned and wiped his nose. "Yeah. Hell yeah, dad. I'm awesome. But why won't you tell Theo?"

"Because he has a big mouth. For now, nobody knows but you. Not even Uncle Dav."

"Wow."

"Yeah. I won't announce it until June or so. That's a long time to keep a secret, but I trust you. There's one more thing. I think it's a bad idea for you to watch the news right now, so I'm going to revoke my permission on that for a few more weeks. I'm not even going to allow myself to watch until this blows over. It's not healthy for either of us. Do you understand?"

Floyd looked deeply disappointed for a moment, but he didn't dwell on it. "Yeah, I guess."

Theo reappeared with the glass of juice and froze by the door, staring uncomprehendingly at the strange sight of his tearful but widely-grinning brother.

"Um. Sorry it took so long. I had to go to the fridge in the pool house." He walked into the room at a glacial pace, talking all the way. "But I told Maurice to put some more in the kitchen. Asked him, I mean. He said he would. Anyway, here you go."

"Thanks," Hank replied as he reached out for the glass. "He's okay, Theody, relax. We were just having a bit of a laugh after all this stress. Floyd, go back to your room and rest before dinner. Come on, up."

"I'm too dizzy," Floyd complained as he struggled against his dad's grip. "Can't I just stay here?"

"Nope. Up you go. Slowly. That's good. You're fine. Into your own bed. Thank you."

Floyd trudged out and Hank watched him disappear into his room, then he turned back to Theo.

"Thanks for your help with his panic attack. I know he appreciated it."

Theo turned his Nintendo back on and flopped onto the bed without making any response.

"You mad at me?" his dad asked after a moment.

"Yep," Theo mumbled.

Hank sighed internally. *What else is new?* he thought dismally. "Okay, well…dinner is in one hour and you know there's no attitude allowed at the table, so either get it out of your system now or forever hold your peace."

"Whatever, dad," Theo replied rudely.

"Wrong answer." Hank strode over and turned off the television with a quick jab to the power button. "Get your butt down to the spare room."

Theo didn't protest for once, and quietly turned off the game and got up. Hank almost felt sorry for him. No, strike that. He *definitely* felt sorry, and quite guilty for keeping such a huge secret from him.

"Wait. Just…never mind. Carry on with your video games. You know where to find me if you need to talk."

Theo didn't even do a double-take at the unprecedented turnaround. He was too tired from today's drama. "Most of the time I *don't* know where to find you, dad. That's why I'm mad."

Hank's heart fell a little. "I'll keep that in mind for the future. See you at dinner."

He fled down the stairs and decided to make an impromptu visit outside to check out the media circus. Avery scrambled up from his little desk in the hallway to accompany him out the front door, sighing inwardly along the way.

There were two state police officers standing on the screened-in porch, somberly guarding the front door like ancient sentinels at an Egyptian tomb. Hank's sudden appearance startled them both, but they quickly recovered.

"How's it going out here?" he asked mildly.

"Good evening, sir. All is well now that we've closed the street all the way to Olympic and Pico. Easy to keep the cars out, but the pedestrians are another matter."

"Hmmm. At least we won't have to worry about them when I move into my new house. The eight-foot walls should see to that."

"When do you move in?" one of the officers asked gingerly.

"Saturday." Hank rested his gaze on the long line of beat-up cars on the street. "Look at all those photographers. Don't know what they're waiting for. It's not like I'm going to stroll out and do a striptease for them."

"No, but maybe you should. It would make everyone forget about your statement pretty quick."

Hank laughed out loud, both at the wisecrack and the horrified expression on the man after he realized what he'd just said.

"Sir, I'm...I'm sorry, that was really-"

Hank waved the mortified apology away, still chuckling at the absurd imagery of the suggestion, then held out his hand. "Hank Bancroft, by the way, as you already know. Thank you for your assistance with this mess. May I ask why the state police are here alongside LAPD? I didn't realize pissing off half the nation would be such a big deal," he joked lightly as he shook their hands, suddenly feeling a lot better about everything.

The one who didn't make the joke said carefully, "There are all kinds of different agencies out here, even animal control." He pointed. "Those guys in green are border patrol from Texas. We're here in Los Angeles for a conference. It was just ending when the all-hands call for this, er, *incident* came through. Sir, it's my pleasure to meet you. I admire the stand you're taking against those horrible measures."

"Me too, sir," said the other officer quickly. As state employees they were not allowed to talk politics while on duty and must register as independents, but this was a human issue more than anything else. Hank felt another surge of joy and relief within his chest.

"Thank you. That's very kind. Where are you boys based?"

"Shasta County, sir."

Well, so much for the warm and fuzzy feeling. Hank's pleasant mood was suddenly overtaken by a dreadful sense of ice encasing his heart, and it didn't help that Avery visibly tensed up beside him.

"I see. Well, thank you for being here, and for your support on the measures."

"Best of luck, sir." *You're going to need it,* his tone said.

"Thank you. Goodnight."

Avery followed him in. "Shasta County, boss?" he hissed.

Hank grimaced as he dug out his phone. "I know. I'm going to take care of that right now."

"Captain Martinez," said the voice on the other side. "Oh, hello Hank. You okay?"

"Good evening. Mind telling me who parked two heavily armed dickheads from an Urbane shithole on my front porch?" he asked with a razor-sharp edge to his tone.

"What?"

"Shasta cops, of all places. Really? Why not Denver? Why not Harmon's own guards? Replace them with LAPD immediately, please."

Martinez sounded a little strangled, like he was trying not to laugh. "I put them there. The red-headed one is my son, and the other is his best friend. Really good eggs, both of them. They're stationed up north temporarily, and they hate it. You're safe."

Hank felt extremely foolish all of a sudden, but it was too late to take back his insults. "Jesus. I'm sorry. How was I supposed to know?"

"When you asked me for protection for your sons, did you really think I'd respond with *heavily armed dickheads from an Urbane shithole?*"

"No, I guess not. Sorry. But you could've given me a heads-up so I wouldn't have a heart attack when I opened the front door."

"Well, I *did* tell you to stay inside, so..."

"You know how well I listen," Hank admitted with an apologetic tenor to his tone.

"Indeed." Martinez grunted. "Can I stop by and talk about this mess in person? I'm actually out in front of Daven's house right now. He just got home, so we're all set here."

Aha...so Dav didn't stay late at the office after all. *He left not even ten minutes after me. Interesting.*

"Yeah, come on by. We're about to have dinner if you want to join. Just try not to say anything that will make my kids shit their pants."

"Fluffy clouds and ponies, got it. I'll be there in a few."

Captain Martinez whistled as Hank played the last of the voicemails for him in the study. There were only fifteen; the inbox had filled up after that. But Hank now had over 4,000 missed calls today. He was surprised the phone hadn't blown up yet.

"Phew. That's some heavy stuff. Don't delete those messages so we can record them at the station tomorrow. You're getting a new number, I take it?"

"Yeah, all of us have to." Just as he said that, the phone rang with another unknown number. He silenced it. "Even Floyd's number got out. You think I have any reason to be worried for my safety?"

"You've got half the nation pissed at you right now, so yes. You might want to consider having two guards with you all the time, instead of just the one. Maybe even a full-fledged police officer or two until this dies down."

"Don't say *dies* , please. And it's hardly half the nation. More like a quarter."

"A third," the captain mused. "At they're not all here in Los Angeles, though. Listen, I'd love to stay for dinner but I have to go check on Rupert and his family now. See you tomorrow?"

Hank's phone screen lit up again, and this time he was surprised to see that it was Harmon.

"Uh, yeah...I think we agreed on nine. I got to take this call, so Avery will walk you out. Thanks, chief."

The two men left, and Hank set down at his desk to answer the call.

"Hank's house of pain, how may I hurt you?"

"Ha, nice," chuckled Harmon.

"Wow, sorry...hope I wasn't on speakerphone," Hank realized belatedly.

"No. Glad to see your sense of humor is still intact after today. Do you have a minute?"

"Yes. What's going on?"

Harmon cleared his throat. "The reaction to your statement is overwhelmingly positive here in Denver. I'm sure it's quite the opposite in Los Angeles."

"You are correct. What do you need?"

"I'm afraid you're not going to like it. Colbert received a call from one of your employees about an hour ago. Said he's pissed about your stance against the party and wanted us to pay him for information on you. Remember the same thing happened to me last month? I don't have a phone number for you or anything, and no clue to his identity, but he said he's pretty high up in the organization."

Hank suddenly felt like vomiting. "Wait, why did Colbert get this call? Why not you?"

"I don't know. Anyway, Hank, we agreed to keep talking to him. To see if we can figure out who he is for you."

"Why would you do that?" Hank asked suspiciously, all alarm bells ringing at the highest volume. "Despite all the niceties lately, have you forgotten we're not exactly friends in this game? And how do I know Colbert isn't just making this up? He hates me."

"I can prove it to you."

"How? Did you record the call?"

"Yes, actually."

Fuck. Hank knew what was coming. A bargain, a blackmail...anything that could make this day worse was just about to happen in the next few seconds.

"Right. So, let me guess: I need to pay or do something in exchange for that recording, and for your assistance in finding out his identity."

"Well, to quote the smartest man I know: have you forgotten we're not exactly friends in this game? Of course there's a price: I want you to stop using double agents, just like I did. You can have the tape, and our cooperation, with a simple agreement on that matter. That's all I ask."

Hank's breathing hitched, and his eyes narrowed so much that he could barely see in front of him.

"No. Never. Are you recording this call, too? You know what, I don't care. We're done. Go fuck yourself. Why don't you go fuck Colbert, too? I know he's there, I can hear his mouth-breathing from here. Although I doubt he'd find any pleasure from your tiny little-"

Harmon's office - Denver

Harmon slammed down the phone and turned to Colbert with a tired shrug as he hit the "stop recording" button on the little black box next to his stapler.

"You happy now?"

"No, boss. That didn't quite go as planned," Colbert responded quietly, although he was silently rejoicing inside. It had gone *exactly* as planned. He wanted Bancroft pissed off at his boss as much as possible.

Harmon sighed heavily. "Right. So much for getting him to stop using double agents now. If that didn't work, nothing will. *Fuck.* Who do you think the caller actually was? Any ideas?"

"No idea," Colbert lied, already itching to call Yannick to congratulate him for being so convincing.

Harmon stood up and stared out his window, feeling depressed and guilty suddenly.

"Send him the tape anyway. Make a copy of it and overnight it."

Colbert's heart almost stopped; if not, then it certainly missed more than a few very important beats. "Wait. What? After what…you just…I don't understand."

"You don't have to understand; it's a direct order. Do it. I want it dropped at FedEx tomorrow by noon. And Colbert? No more of these games. I understand what happened tonight, but I need him on my good side. I know you hate him, and you have to put that aside or else we're going to have a serious problem. I'm going home."

Bancroft House

Hank was so angry about Harmon's call that he could barely stomach the idea of food as he sat down at the table with Avery and his sons - well, one of them, anyway. Theo hadn't shown up yet.

"Floyd, go get your brother," Hank ordered at 7:02pm. He didn't tolerate his kids being late for anything, and this would lead to a chat in the study if there wasn't a good excuse for Theo's tardiness.

Floyd flew up the stairs, and Hank turned to Avery. "Hey, what did you think about the chief's suggestion that we have a couple real police officers hanging around here for a while? I don't think it's a bad idea. I mean, we're down one guard anyway."

"Agreed. Why don't you ask him about those two on the front porch? Sounds like they want to get away from Shasta, and this could be a good excuse to get them out."

"Hmmm. Good idea. Did you send me the new policy?"

"Fifteen minutes after you asked me for it, yes. To your personal email. Once you approve it, I'll post it downstairs. You okay, boss? You seem...you look red."

"I wish I could explain, I really do. But it's a party matter. Internal thing. I need to talk to Daven."

"Not to pry, but...are you even on speaking terms right now?"

"Your guess is as good as mine."

They waited a few more minutes, and Hank got up to venture to Theo's room. He and Floyd were arguing, and Hank didn't need to hear what it was all about. He already knew Theo was still pouting and trying to make a statement, and Floyd was trying to convince him otherwise.

"...not that big of a deal, please. Don't get him mad. He's had a horrible day. Come on!"

They turned as Hank entered the room. "Floyd, downstairs."

"Dad, please don't, he's just upset about...a lot."

"I know. Move."

He crossed his arms and waited until Floyd was out of earshot. "Theo, you have to eat. If you think I'm going to just let you stay up here and-"

"I don't care what you do anymore," Theo replied angrily, flopping himself down on his bed.

"You have exactly one more chance to obey me. I'm going to count to five."

He got to four before Theo flung himself back on his feet and angrily stomped down the stairs. Once he got to the table, however, he was angelic and quiet. Floyd watched them both with wide eyes as they ate in silence. Normally, their dad would be chatting throughout the entire meal and asking everyone questions about their day, and pulling out answers from them that they were holding back. He was a veritable master at table conversation.

Tonight, however, he didn't say a word.

CHAPTER SIX

Bancroft House #2 - Los Angeles

Hank Bancroft was exhausted and terribly sick. The past 16 days had stretched his stamina and patience to the limits. Not only was he dealing with the backlash of his own party, but he had also moved into a new house, ignored Harmon and Stewart to the point of being summoned to Philadelphia, was nearly forced to fire Taylor for an inadvertent information leak (Hank sorely wished the "reply all" option could be removed from email altogether), and had been obliged to take the increasingly rebellious Theo into his new study almost every day. He was at wits' end with the boy.

There were a few bright spots. Floyd had been unusually angelic and encouraging, and Rupert not far behind...but it wasn't enough. The rest of shit he was putting up with was too much, and coupled with Daven's inexplicable coldness towards him lately, Hank was skirting the edge of multiple breakdowns.

The March 1 vote was occurring today, and by noon he found himself quarantined in his home with a sore throat so severe he could not speak at all. Even worse, he couldn't keep his eyes open long enough to read and reply to emails. The only person who would visit him now was Rupert, who had already gone through the same strain of flu and considered himself immune to getting it again. Hank prayed he was right, and he had rarely prayed for anything before.

"Hey, Hank, can I come in?" Rupert called from the bedroom door when he visited after work. Then, remembering Hank couldn't speak, he let himself in. "Shake your head if you want me to leave. No? Okay. I brought you some green tea."

Now Hank shook his head.

"Sorry, just a little joke. It's a London Fog with lavender, naturally. Your chef spent many dramatic minutes putting it together, so try to pretend you like it. What day are you due to go to Philadelphia?"

Hank held up three fingers.

"March 3? Yeah, no way. Look at you. Want me to call Stewart?"

Hank nodded after significant hesitation, and Rupert took a deep breath as he pulled out his phone.

"Stewart? I'm sorry to call so late. This is Rupert Aster, on behalf of Hank Bancroft. Yes, you too, thank you. I'm with Hank. He's too ill to come to Philadelphia on Friday. May we-"

There was a long pause, and Rupert looked puzzled through most of it. "But he, he can't...he can't speak or work right now, I assure you. His temperature is almost 103. You what?......no, that's not acceptable, I'm sorry."

Hank was so drained that he didn't care what proposal of Stewart's that Rupe considered acceptable or not, and he let his friend fight for him without trying to intervene. In fact, he could just drift off to sleep right now. *Yes, that would be really nice* . He started to slip out of consciousness a little, Rupert's angry but level words blurring together into a not unpleasant droning noise. In and out, in and out, until he could hear his blood rushing and feel his heart beating. Then the lights and sound inside his head went out altogether.

When Hank awoke again, it was pitch black outside and Rupert was asleep on the sofa on the other side of the room. He tried to call out for him, but no sound emerged, so Hank picked up the remote control for his television and aimed to throw it against the wall.

Unfortunately he had no strength, and the remote made it all of four feet away from the bed, with nary a thump on the thick carpet.

So Hank closed his eyes and went back to sleep again. This time, he woke to a doctor hovering over him, with Rupert pacing in the background.

"What the-" he tried, to no avail.

"You're alright, Mr. Bancroft. It's Doctor Milligan. I work at Palisades Hospital and you've seen me once before."

Hank looked at Rupert and held up three fingers again, with an accompanying quizzical expression.

"Yes, it took some wrangling but Stewart agreed to postpone until March 10. You're all set."

The three fingers changed to a thumbs-up, and then Hank tapped his wrist. Someone had taken his watch off.

"It's just after 5am," the doctor replied casually. "You're going to be alright in about a week. It's unusual to have such a severe strain of this flu in healthy, strong men like you, but you've been under a tremendous amount of stress. But I can-"

"The vote," Hank rasped desperately.

The doctor ignored that. "I can assure you that you won't see the end of the week if you don't get hydrated. Since you can't keep anything down, we need to move you to the hospital now."

"Obviously a good idea, but how are we going to manage it without an ambulance, and without the press getting into a feeding frenzy?" queried Rupert gloomily. They continued the discussion turned away from the bed in order to diplomatically ignore Hank's silent, writhing protest.

"The...vote..." he croaked in vain.

Rupert turned back around after a few minutes and swallowed hard. "Listen, you got to go to the hospital. I insist, no arguing."

"No, no, and no. Fuck you," Hank whispered slowly and painfully.

"Alrighty, then." Rupert let out a resigned sigh and looked at the doctor. "That's that. Hell will have to literally freeze over before this man agrees to go to the hospital. You've got to do your thing here."

"Alright. Then I have to call my tech in, and a nurse."

"Do it," Rupe said with finality. He didn't look at Hank as he left the room and went into the hallway. Floyd and Theo were both standing there, looking pale and scared.

"Hey guys. Good news, he's going to be fine. It's just the flu. I had it too, though not as bad. We're calling in a nurse to help him out for a few days and stay with him. Go back to bed, and after breakfast I want you each to pack a bag for Daven's house so you don't risk getting this thing, too. You're probably have to stay over for four or five days."

"Can't we stay with you?" Floyd asked quietly, and it was nothing against Daven. Just that it would be easier, since their school was in the same house.

"Unfortunately not. You know Dav is your legal guardian when Hank is unavailable."

"I know, but-"

" *No* , and don't ask me again. Back to bed, both of you."

For a moment Floyd was going to protest, but he took another look at Rupert's no-nonsense determination and wisely changed his mind. When the boys had gone, Rupe reluctantly went back into Hank's room.

"Okay, boss. While we wait for the nurse, I'm going to tell you about the vote." He looked meaningfully at Doctor Milligan, who picked up his chart and left the room.

"Well?" Hank queried in a rasp once the door had closed.

"Public flogging didn't pass. It was close, nearly a tie. All your long nights of writing and giving all those fiery speeches paid off, against all odds. Congratulations, Hank."

"Motherfucker," Hank muttered, unable to celebrate the win because he already realized that Rupert was cheerfully giving him the good news first in order to prepare him for the bad.

"What was that?" Rupe asked, genuinely not having understood the comment.

"Nothing. And?"

"I can't understand what you're saying, so I'll just continue. You already knew that the other one really had no hope of failing. Too many of the elite independents supported it, and in the end it wasn't even close. Even a large swath of Urbanes voted for it, which is a surprise."

Hank nodded, feeling sick to his stomach now on top of everything else. The measures to toughen up the parameters of indentured servitude and sentence the children of felons to such a life was about to become reality. And that, in part, was caused by the Seditionist's past stances on other related issues. Everything was cause and effect in politics, but had Hank foreseen this development, he never would have supporting cutting back on undocumented day laborers seven years ago.

Rupert pulled up a chair and sat next to his beloved boss, who was staring blankly at the ceiling. Gently he said, "I know what you're thinking, Hank. But please stop. We couldn't have predicted this back when we supported other measures that indirectly led up to it. This is never what we wanted. I'm going to take advantage of the fact that you can't speak right now, which means you can't argue with me, and I'm going to tell you something I've always wanted to say. You are a good man. Everything you've ever done - in your entire life - was for a good reason and for the greater good of all. The sacrifices you've made, the endless strategizing, the long hours, the writing, the speaking...none of it will be in vain because of one wrong measure."

"Four," Hank croaked. He was referring to this one, and the three that he had failed to stop last year.

"Leave it to you to argue even in this condition. Four, then. Out of how many? Listen, I'm not going to put up with you feeling sorry for yourself over this. Neither will Daven. Your conscience should be clear because you truly did the best you could to prevent this outcome. I mean...look at you right now, you've nearly killed yourself trying to do the right thing. But when you're better, we move on, and we do bigger and greater right things. Do I have your agreement?"

"No. I'm done," Hank declared with finality.

Rupert paused, his heart going into a freefall at the words. *I'm done...* and he obviously didn't mean he was dying. He meant he was done as leader of the party. Quitting.

He meant it, too.

"I'm sorry, Hank, still can't understand you. Rest your throat, and I'll...uh, the nurse should be here very soon. I'm going to check on the boys and call the doctor in for you. Be right back."

He fled the room and went outside, where the new red-headed guard and his friend were keeping station on the porch. The street was nearly empty except for one lone photographer's car, and the sun was just rising enough to show a streak of purple over the treetops.

"How's he doing, sir?" Martinez inquired.

"Don't call me sir, please. I'm Rupert, or Mr. Aster if you prefer. In about half an hour there will be a nurse and a medical technician arriving from Palisades hospital. Let them in once the doctor comes down and identifies them, not before."

"Yes, sir...Mr. Aster. How is he?"

Rupert wasn't trying to be evasive by not telling them how Hank was; he actually didn't hear the question at all amongst his racing thoughts. "Thank you. I'm going home, and I'll be back at 7 to have breakfast with the boys."

The guards nodded, and Rupe got into his car with a heavy heart.

——

Seditionists HQ - later that morning

"Dav, we got to talk," said Rupe gloomily as his colleague and friend entered the office an hour late, due to the unexpected arrival of Hank's boys at his front door first thing in the morning.

"About what?"

"In your office? Thanks."

Rupert made himself a cup of coffee before going into the office and closing the door firmly behind him. Daven was scowling and rifling through his briefcase, not looking up.

"Dav...I'm sorry for springing Hank's boys on you this morning. I really am, and I should have given you more notice. But I must say, I'm really disappointed at the way you handled it and how rude you were to all of us. Hank chose you as their guardian for a reason. What the hell is going on with you lately?"

"I don't want to talk about it," Dav said as he slammed his briefcase shut.

"I don't care. Talk about it anyway, or I'm going to make Hank wring it out of you when he gets back. Or I will, right now. You're being a total dick to everyone, and people are starting to talk."

Daven hung up his coat, then took a minute to dig out a file from somewhere deep within his closet.

"Fine. You asked for it. Here you go."

He all but threw the file to Rupe, who took it with dismayed astonishment and started flipping through it with increasing alarm.

"What the... *where* did you get this? Is this for real?"

"Appears to be. They came in the mail to my house just after the audit that uncovered them."

Rupe felt sicker and sicker as he studied the six receipts for a third, and then a fourth time.

"Holy shit, Dav. He *did* pay those fuckers off. Son of a bitch . Who sent these to you?"

"No idea. Came in regular mail, and the zip code it was sent from was our own. Somebody within our organization, probably."

"And you haven't done anything about it?"

Daven walked over and snatched the papers back. "Obviously not!"

Rupert wandered over to Daven's desk chair and collapsed into it. Hank was going to have a stroke over Dav hiding this development for so long, there was no doubt of it. "Fuck. What are you going to do?"

"Talk to him. I've been waiting until after the vote to do it, because we needed him focused on that. It gets worse. He allegedly offered Colton Gamble money for his help with passing his photography measure. Don't ask me how I found out, because I'm not proud of it. And don't even get me started on this infatuation with Harmon. I'm about ten seconds away from quitting every time I think about how he let the Janet investigation get buried just to win some bread points with the Urbanes."

"It's *brownie* points, Dav. Shit. Well, he's too sick to confront now. It would probably kill him to have an argument. You'll have to wait."

"I will. But if these are only little things I'm uncovering by chance, or by someone else exposing them, this could only be scratching the surface. Who knows what else he's up to?"

Rupert gaped at Daven as if he was on fire. "Do you remember what happened in December when we assumed the same thing over one single call? We were completely wrong about all of it, and we nearly lost our jobs to boot. This is Hank we're talking about. Hank *Bancroft* . We're godfathers to his children. Don't paint him in some ridiculous, nefarious light. There's going to be a good explanation, just like last time."

"Right. And the explanation will be: sorry guys, let me explain. I lied, and I really did pay them off ."

"Jesus, Dav. Don't get all high and mighty on me. If he did this - which we don't know for sure - he was desperately trying to protect his sons. Don't you understand? And in the end, it's truly just his problem, not ours. He's going to be the one who has to dig himself out of this."

"Except that he used Seditionists funds to do it, and the money was allocated from my department. So no, it's not *just* his problem. It's now mine, too. So don't tell me what to do, or how I should feel about being lied to!"

Daven was all but over the conversation, but as they were in his office, there was nowhere to go. They were both silent for a minute after that statement, fuming and nearly ready to physically fight each other for the first time since they'd known each other. It took all of Rupert's willpower not to stomp out of the office, but something was holding him back from doing that.

Then he realized what was really bothering him. He had been completely wrong to blindly defend Hank in the face of such evidence, and in the presence of a man who stood to lose so much from it. He should have had Daven's back on this one, and he failed him completely.

Rupe's voice was tight and full of emotion. "Dav...I'm sorry. You're right. I didn't mean to be flippant. I support you. Please forgive me. What's your next step? Is there anything I can do for you right now?"

Daven took a huge swig from one of the comically small water bottles he always kept in his coat pocket. "Thank you, and I accept your apology. Do you have a suggestion on how to proceed with some kind of investigation that we can keep hidden from Hank?"

"First we polygraph the entire accounting department and find out who made those payments. He was expecting that, anyway. And let's hope he doesn't come back too soon. We already poly'd Yannick, so I'll start with the other senior employees right away. This afternoon. With your permission, of course."

Daven looked at him sideways. "My what?"

"You're the big boss man while Hank's away. What say you?"

"Yes, proceed. You have my express authorization to do whatever you need to get it done quickly and efficiently."

Rupert rolled his eyes as he turned to leave the office. "Yes, sir, right away, sir."

"Thank you."

Daven didn't get home until almost 9pm, and he and Lucas found the boys sitting on the couch half-asleep, with Brittany sitting nearby reading the newspaper. It was the evening edition, in which Hank's illness was exaggerated and splashed all over the local section's headlines.

"Did you have dinner?" Daven asked all three of them at large, casting a wary eye on their guard, who got the message and subtly flipped the newspaper over on the table to hide its contents.

Theo nodded. "Yeah. How's dad?"

"The same. Your bedtime is 9:30pm, so why don't you get ready for that. Sorry I'm back so late. Without your dad at the office things can get a little hectic. Brittany, can I talk to you for a minute?"

The boys went back to their rooms, and Brittany and Daven went into the kitchen.

"I haven't even had time to ask about Hank today, or to even think about him," Daven admitted tiredly. "Have you heard anything?"

"Yes, I'm up to date as of about twenty minutes ago. High fever, very sleepy, can't talk. Nothing has changed. Everyone else seems fine in the house, and they've sterilized it top to bottom a few times today."

"Okay. Are Theo and Floyd behaving?"

"Theo's been a handful. I think his dad would have had a word with him about two hours ago for the way he was talking to me and his brother, but other than that everything's fine."

Daven nodded. "Thanks. Are you staying here?"

"That's up to you. I can if you want me to, and I wouldn't mind staying away from the plague house."

"That's fine, take the bedroom next to mine. It has its own bathroom. Thanks for your help."

Daven started with his nightly routine of doing random things around the house and was about to wish the boys goodnight when he heard them arguing loudly. With a deep sigh he made his way upstairs with Shannon close on his heels as the noise escalated while they argued about who could use the shower first. He was tired and didn't have time for this, but he couldn't exactly blow it off and hope for the best.

"Boys," he called calmly as he entered the bedroom they shared. "Come out here, please."

The noise abruptly stopped. Shannon jumped onto one of the beds and made herself comfortable while Floyd emerged first from the bathroom, with Theo close behind him. Dav was used to having Hank's sons argue around him (since they couldn't do it in front of their dad), and he had learned from years of experience how to intimidate them into silence without having to resort to making threats. All he had to do was cross his arms and look down at them disapprovingly.

"What's the solution to this problem?" he asked. Classic Daven - straight to the point.

"There's no problem, Uncle Dav," Floyd replied quickly. "We were just both trying to be first to use the bathroom." Theo stayed silent, thankfully.

"Do I need to decide anything for you in regards to that, or can you work it out on your own?"

"Theo can go first, it's no big deal. Everything's fine, Uncle Dav."

"Good. Proceed, then. My bedroom is right across the hall, as you know, and I prefer to sleep without being awakened by loud voices. Can I count on you to let me do that?"

They both nodded, eyes wide. Daven's tone was kind and friendly, and although the boys knew he would never lash out in anger or lay a hand on them, they wouldn't disobey him now if someone offered them a million bucks to do it. Their father often privately bemoaned his inability to have the same effect on them, much to Daven's embarrassment.

"Okay, then. I'm going to bed. As you know, you're not to leave this room for any reason until I open the door in the morning." That was only because they would likely wake Shannon up and incite a flurry of frantic barking. She was an excellent guard dog, if a bit overzealous. All of Daven's guards and regular visitors had gotten on his bad side at least once for making too much noise in the middle of the night and setting her off.

"Shannon, come along. Off the bed. Good girl. Goodnight, boys."

"Goodnight," they said together. The bedroom door closed, and Floyd turned and quietly but firmly shoved Theo to the floor.

"Bitch!" he hissed.

"Idiot!" Theo whispered back.

The door opened back up again and Daven peeked in.

"Oh, I forgot to tell you..." he watched in dismay as Theo scrambled off the floor and back onto his feet. Floyd cleared his throat, trying to get out some kind of reasonable explanation, but there was none. Anyone with eyes and a brain could gather what had just happened.

"Come here, Floyd," he said gravely, and Floyd obediently followed Daven into the hallway with a look of deep regret and shame on his face.

"You know what your father would do if he saw what I just saw, right?"

"Yes. I'm sorry."

"You're sixteen years old, beating up on a twelve year old, in my house. That's not acceptable, and your dad will be hearing about it when he's recovered. Go apologize to Theo, and then go to bed. Clear?"

Floyd nodded, eyes wide and wet. He hated disappointing people, especially Daven, and this was the first time he had ever had a reason to rebuke him in this manner. It hurt, and it was embarrassing.

"Do you have to tell him?" he tried, hoping desperately for a reprieve.

"I'm not going to tell him. You are, when he asks you if you behaved yourself. What I was going to say earlier is that I forgot to tell you both that school will start late tomorrow because Mrs. Aster has an appointment. We'll go out for breakfast at a restaurant, then take Shannon to the dog park. Brittany will wake you guys up at 8."

Floyd wiped his eyes with the sleeve of his sweatshirt and composed himself again. "Okay. That sounds nice."

Daven nodded, then reached out and patted a shoulder in what he hoped was a reassuring manner, but it felt more awkward than anything else. "See you in the morning. Goodnight."

By the end of day two, Rupe was starting to make himself crazy with the possibilities behind the receipts Daven had received. He even started talking to himself to keep track of his thoughts and bullet points.

Guilty of not covering his tracks properly....

That is so unlike you, Hank - the smartest man I've ever known. The most manipulative and careful man I've ever known. You've never missed a detail nor ever forgot them.

Which by itself alone argued for his innocence, because he wouldn't be that dumb. But then again, Hank had offered said bribes to Urbanes photographers on live television, with his son and a very angry Daven in tow.

Jesus, Hank. Maybe you really are that dumb. I mean, you did threaten Harmon on live television. Twice.

Putting everyone's careers on the line by using Seditionist Funds...

He would never put Daven's career on the line. Or mine. Never. But then again, he did nearly fire us for taking phone calls on Christmas eve, and then publicly shamed us for it...

The money was allocated from Daven's department....

That could have been a mistake. Errors in coding happen all the time amongst the more inexperienced bookkeepers...but, those with access to the anonymous account were highly experienced.

Back to square one again: Hank is paying off bribes with company funds and leaving a trail behind that leads straight to him.

...which would mean he's all but lost his mind, and I'm not willing to accept that.

If Hank intended to make an illegal bribe, why would he not use private funds instead?

...because personal banks do not allow anonymous ledger entries. It would have been too traceable.

And why the hell would he offer money to Colton Gamble to help pass that measure?

... desperation. Needed to save your boys from the press. Floyd's panic attacks becoming more frequent.

Colton Gamble had worked for Harmon once.

... Yes. Colton Gamble worked for Harmon once. Is that important? Is that a thing?

No, they had a falling out. Harmon hates Colton Gamble. They aren't even on speaking terms.

...but Colton Gamble is best friends with Colbert.

And Colbert hates Hank Bancroft.

Irrelevant. They've always hated each other, so why would Colbert start something now? And what would Colton Gamble have to gain?

Who sent the receipts?

An inside man. We'll never know, because we can't ask that question during the polygraph. It will expose Hank's crime. Or...not crime..or....fuck it all.

Rupe threw down his notebook and called Daven. "I've got nothing, Dav. I keep going in circles."

"I'm coming over."

Thirty seconds later they were face to face again.

"I have nothing, either," Dav admitted. "If anything, I'm more convinced he did it. At least Hank is still too sick to come in, or do much at all. Let's just hope he stays that way for another few days, or preferably until we can put him going off to Philadelphia next week."

The men looked at each other, horrified that they were on the same wavelength and harboring such dark thoughts.

"I didn't mean..."

"It's okay, Dav. I've been thinking the same: as long as he stays deathly ill, that gives us more time to save him. God help us..."

CHAPTER SEVEN

Saturday morning, March 4.

Daven's House

Daven was not used to having a full table at breakfast in his house - usually he dined alone at all meals - but he thought it was something he could probably get used to and enjoy. It wasn't planned, either, and just kind of happened as more people showed up at the house all at the same time. The boys were there, of course, and Brittany, Lucas, Rupert, and even Captain Martinez, who had stopped by to follow up on a report that someone was climbing over the back fence of the property. There were clear indications of someone trying to do that, but the officers had concluded the attempt was unsuccessful.

Daven had agreed to the boys' request to fix breakfast, much to his current regret. Theo was busy making a colossal mess with the waffle iron, and Daven had to almost physically hold himself back from trying to help him and prevent more mess. Theo had even spilled an entire carton of orange juice all over the floor in a moment of carelessness. As a neat freak, it had nearly pushed Daven over the edge, but he kept quiet.

Floyd, on the other hand, expertly cooked and served everyone oatmeal, sausage, and eggs, as well as pouring all the drinks and setting the table. He was obviously thoroughly enjoying himself and the company, and was happier than Dav had seen him all week.

As Theo slid a grossly deformed but perfectly cooked waffle in front of the very grateful police captain, Rupe finally put two and two together in regards to the man's last name.

"Are you related to Hank's new guard, by chance? He's a Deveraux, too if I'm not mistaken."

The captain reached for the syrup and smiled broadly. "My son. Thank god for Hank's intervention on that one."

Daven cocked his head curiously. "Oh? Was he previously unemployed for some time?"

"No, not at all. Worked as a state police officer and was transferred to Shasta six months ago, against his will. Toby went with him - that's his best friend since they were babies, practically - to make it more bearable. But it wasn't enough. I casually mentioned to Hank they hated it up there, then went on my way and forgot we ever had the conversation."

Rupe grunted. "Going from Los Angeles to Shasta County? What a grisly downgrade."

"That's why they can't keep any Southern California boys up there on a long-term basis and have to force them into it. Only thing it's got going for it is a big-ass lake that you can't even fish in anymore because of the tree-hugging plagues of Urbanes."

Daven asked, "So Hank had them transferred back to LAPD?"

"No. Not even two hours after hearing how unhappy they were - didn't even ask questions - he simply went out on the porch, sipping a beer, and asked them to join his own guards. Just like that. Offered a shit ton of money for 'em, too, didn't even try to bargain. The boys got back home a few days ago, pinching themselves daily and still not quite believing it all. Needless to say, their kids and wives are over the moon to have him home three days a week." He looked at Floyd and smiled. The teenager had sat down earlier to enjoy his own food but was now frozen still, fully enraptured by the tale he was hearing.

"He did that, sir?"

"He didn't tell you? Guess I'm not surprised. Your dad is a pain in the ass more often than not, but he's a good man. The best kind of man there is, and I'll fight anyone who says otherwise." He turned his attention back to Rupe and Dav. "It pisses me off, all the shit headlines he's been getting recently. Doesn't deserve any of 'em."

"Language, please," said Daven gently, cocking his head subtly towards the boys.

"Right. Sorry."

"We don't give a fuck about bad words," Theo piped up cheerfully from his station in the kitchen. Everyone at the table gasped, and then roared. Except Daven, of course. He smiled thinly, then stood up and went into the kitchen while everyone else continued to laugh and make conversation.

"How's it going over here, Theo? Making a mess, I see."

"I'm trying not to, Uncle Dav. Kept putting too much batter in, but I think I've got it now."

"Good. Remember that I told you there's no swearing in my house. Don't do it again, please."

"You swear all the time in your house," Theo replied cheekily, his grin indicating he meant no harm and had no intention of arguing any further. No, he was only basking in the attention from the crowd. The same type of positive and encouraging attention he didn't get very often from his father.

Daven gave in without a fight and reached way up into the cupboard to grab two more rolls of paper towels. "I guess you're right. Clean this shit up when you're done."

"I will. This waffle iron is going to be a bitch to clean."

"Let it cool down first, it's hot as fuck right now."

Theo giggled, and Daven opened the fridge, deeply depressed about the story Captain Martinez had just told. How he said he would fight anyone who didn't consider Hank a good man.

The words were strikingly familiar; Daven had once felt the same way. Just...not lately. And why not? He deeply admired Hank's huge balls in standing against his own party, was constantly moved by his rousing speeches given to hostile crowds that were quickly won over, and had been touched by the countless other good and positive things Hank had done for his constituents and even his opponents. For his friends. For complete strangers, like Martinez. Hell, the man had even ditched all his responsibilities in order to pursue Shannon around the city for hours, even though his friendship with Dav had already come to a certain end.

Somehow, Dav had forgotten Hank's true nature, and he suddenly hated himself for it. What's worse, it was his own fault. He was still bitterly hung up on the ugly consequences of the Christmas Day fiasco, even though he should be thankful Hank didn't fire him on the spot.

Even after Dav and Rupe had clearly proven they couldn't be trusted, Hank trusted them again anyway - after a few weeks of tension and petty bickering, to be sure - but he eventually forgave and let them back in, because that's the kind of man he was to his friends.

And what kind of friend am I being to him right now?

Dav continued to gather his thoughts while pretending to search for something in the fridge, then caught Rupert's eye as he grabbed the nearest bottle of what looked like root beer and sat back down. It was clear they were both thinking exactly the same thing.

We need to talk to him, Rupert's eyes said.

Daven nodded, then turned his attention to his cold, mangled waffle.

"Are you really going to put barbecue sauce on your waffle, Uncle Dav?" Theo asked in awe.

Bancroft House

Afternoon, same day

"Hey, boss," Rupert said quietly as he entered Hank's room with a bag of takeout from The Daily Grill. He hoped he could entice Hank to eat, but the odds seemed dismal; two other plates of uneaten food were already on the nightstand.

"Hey," Hank replied sleepily. "You're late. Can you close the curtains?"

"Sorry. Got caught in traffic." That was a feeble joke; Rupe only lived four blocks away. He walked around the room shutting the blackout curtains, which were so effective even in the middle of the day that he had to follow Hank's voice to make his way back to him.

"How are you doing?"

"Can't talk much. Hot. Nauseated. Annoyed."

"I'm sure. Stopped at your favorite place to grab you a chicken pot pie, despite my wife's insistence that it was too much for you to handle right now. It appears she's right. Again."

"Thank you, but you need to call me when you're going to be late, even if I am on my deathbed."

Oh…that's why he was annoyed.

"I apologize, Hank. Won't happen again. And you're hardly on your deathbed."

"Feels like it. Can you get Dav on speakerphone now, please? I want to get this over with."

Rupert flipped open his phone and realized with a start that he was almost 40 minutes late. Shit, he'd really lost track of time. Hank was still his boss no matter what, and this was a business meeting - one that Rupe himself had requested, and that Hank had agreed to despite his illness.

"Doing it now. I'm sorry," he repeated again, feeling like a complete dick as he dialed. The light from the phone enabled him to spot a chair in the corner, and he dragged it over next to the bed during the veritable eternity it took for Dav to pick up. Once he did, Rupert carefully laid the phone next to Hank so they could both hear and speak into it.

"Hello Rupert," Dav said robotically. "May I assume Hank is on the line as well?"

"Present, Mr. Johansson."

Oh boy…Hank was in a mood now. This couldn't be good. Rupert braced himself, already feeling overly emotional in advance from the epic argument he thought was inevitable.

"Alright, Dav. Since you volunteered to go first, please tell him from the beginning what we called this meeting for."

"Can't wait," Hank grumbled.

Daven took a deep breath. "Hank, I know this is going to be very upsetting. Please stay calm and let us talk this through from all points of view. I recently received a packet in the mail that implicates you in a bribery scheme. It was a packet of what appear to be original receipts for six payments made to Urbane photographers under your name."

Hank started to sit up, which knocked the phone onto the floor and popped it shut. "What!"

Rupe put a firm hand on his shoulder as he reached down to fumble for his cell in the pitch dark. "Hank, please. Just listen. Lay down. We'll explain everything. Try not to get agitated."

"Easy for you to say!"

"None of this is easy for me!" Rupe snapped back harshly as he found the phone and re-dialed Dav as quickly as his trembling fingers could manage. It was the first time he could ever recall talking back to Hank in that manner, and it rattled him. He was relieved when Daven picked up on the first ring.

"Sorry about that, Dav. Technical difficulty. Go ahead."

Dav continued as if he had never stopped. "We've been investigating them for several days to determine where they came from and who forged them. So far we haven't found the hard evidence we need to prove they're fakes. Whoever did this was on the inside, since everything lines up with our accounting and the timeline of the payments down to the minute. There's no external party who has access to that information. But no one in accounting has yet failed a polygraph test designed to figure out who made the payments. Do you have any idea of who might be behind this?"

Hank was probably white as a sheet, but it was too dark for Rupert to see him. He made no response, but tensed up enough that the bed moved slightly.

"Hank?" Rupert gently prodded.

"How long...when did you get this package?"

"Three weeks ago. I only told Rupert on Wednesday, and we've been working frantically since then."

Why the fuck did you wait? Hank wanted to ask, but he refrained because he already knew the very uncomfortable answer.

"Okay. And what have you discovered so far?"

"The payments were made by cashier's check, likely bought in person. If we can determine where they were purchased, we might be able to obtain security footage and interview the person, or persons, who sold them. If we can confirm even one person who was paid with them, Stewart can issue a subpoena for a deposition."

"That's a lot of ifs. And a subpoena requires an indictment first, Dav," Hank said wearily. He was getting sleepy again, despite the shock of this news and the initial adrenaline rush.

"I believe Stewart can authorize a special investigation to prevent that. You'll have to ask him. Anyway, we have a handwriting professional coming in on Monday morning to analyze your signature versus those on the documents. We're already a quarter of the way through polygraphing our accountants. Lastly, we want to pull phone records to determine what calls were made between Colton Gamble and Harmon, and to see what evidence can be gathered from those."

"Colton Gamble? Why?"

Rupe jumped in now, his heart pounding with a sick, deep thudding against his ribs. "He says you offered him money to help push your measure through the house."

"For fuck's sake. No, I did not."

"Is there a recording of your call with him?" Rupe eventually asked, after a long silence from Dav.

"Calls, plural. We had about seven. No, because they were between our cell phones."

Rupe felt like crying, he was that frustrated right now at Hank's refusal to use his office phone for these calls so that could be recorded. They had had the argument countless times before.

Dav continued now. "Okay, well…then there's no evidence, and Stewart will have to let that go. In regards to the receipts, there's no way to complete the investigation before you go to Philadelphia. We can't finish polygraphing the entire accounting department that quickly."

"And the tape?" Hank was rapidly losing his voice again, and the question came out as a whisper.

"Yes, regarding the tape we got from Harmon. That's next on my list to discuss. The voice analysis is due back Thursday, despite our rush job. They had quite a back-up at the lab we contract with, and no other lab is trustworthy enough to handle it because we didn't have time to vet them."

"Hmmm."

"Have you spoken to Harmon since we got it?"

"No. You know that."

Another long silence. Rupe and Dav were intensely curious why Hank was so pissed off at Harmon, especially considering the man had provided something to them for free that was incredibly valuable, but neither one of them had taken the precarious step towards asking Hank about it yet. He would tell them if and when he needed to.

"I'm really tired, guys. I need to go back to sleep. Proceed however you feel is best."

Daven paused. "Well, we would like to get your permission first to look into a few other possibilities. Today I was thinking of-"

"Not necessary. Do whatever you need to do."

Dav should have liked that answer, but he didn't. "Okay, are you just saying that because you're sick and don't have the energy to deal with this? Because that's not like you, and I'm not comfortable having free rein like this. I want to make sure you-"

"Sounds like you've managed fine on your own so far. Why stop now?"

There was an ugly but understandable bitterness to that remark. Hank had clearly reached his wits' end with today's news. Rupe hadn't forgotten his friend's vow that he was "done" with his job. Even though Rupe had pretended not to hear him at the time, and it hadn't come up again. But the memory of that remark upset him far more than he was comfortable admitting to himself.

"Thank you for your trust, Hank," Rupe said once he recovered his own wits. "You have our word that we're doing everything in our power to get to the bottom of this. We won't stop until you're completely cleared and all the questions are answered."

"I already know the answer," declared Hank tiredly. "Colbert is behind this."

"Most likely," murmured Rupert.

"We have him on our list of possibilities," Dav admitted. "But there's no evidence yet."

"There will be." Hank replied. "His best friend is Colton Gamble, and you know I don't believe in coincidences."

"We're exploring that angle. But it almost seems too obvious, don't you think? Everyone knows you hate each other, and that he's practically in Gamble's back pocket. He would have to know he'd be the very first suspect. And why would he want to start something with you now, after all these years? There are others with much more to gain from your downfall."

"Rupe and I know Colbert intimately. You don't. This is all him, and he's an impatient, arrogant bastard who will step on his own dick soon enough. That's when the red flags will start flying left and right. Keep your eyes open. I'm going back to bed, so let's end this for now."

"He's right about Colbert, Dav. I'll come by your house in a few minutes," said Rupe. He hung up the phone and turned to his best friend of ten years, feeling like the worst piece of shit on the planet.

"I'm sorry to have ambushed you with this while you're so sick, but I had no choice. You need to talk to the FBI on Monday. Or maybe Tuesday, depending on the results of the signature analysis."

"I forgive you for thinking I did it, Rupe," Hank said quietly. Peacefully, even.

"What? I never thought that."

"Don't lie," Hank murmured quietly. "I know you. I know the signs of guilt in your voice, in your eyes."

"My eyes, huh? It's pitch black in here, Hank." Rupert felt like crying, and his voice wavered with the guilt that Hank apparently knew so well. Damn it.

"Just admit it, it's alright," Hank added sleepily.

Rupert cleared his throat roughly. "I really need to get going so I can keep working on this with Dav, but I'd like to come by again after church tomorrow if that's okay. To see how you're doing and give you an update on the boys."

"Yes, please. I might ask you to heat up that pot pie for me, too." The bed rustled as Hank shifted slightly, and Rupert felt a burning hot palm rest on his forearm. "Whatever changed your mind, don't let anything change it back. I may be an ornery, impulsive fucker sometimes, and intolerable the rest of the time...but I don't lie to my friends."

That was all it took for Rupe's eyes to start leaking. "I know, Hank," he managed to get out. "I'm so sorry."

"It's okay. Go. See you tomorrow."

Hank patted Rupe's arm once, then slid his hand away and closed his eyes. Rupert wiped his sleeve across his wet face, and reluctantly left his friend.

"Goddamn, that was utterly agonizing," complained Rupert bitterly as he strolled through the front door of Daven's house and threw down his keys on the sideboard. "Would rather have had my-"

"Keep your voice down. Theo and Floyd are having lunch in the dining room. Come to my study."

They went in, and Daven poured Rupert a huge shot of bourbon without asking.

"He knows we thought he did it, Dav."

"Yes. He handled it all fairly well, considering."

Rupert held out his glass for a refill of bourbon, but Daven didn't oblige.

"No, I need you to be clear-headed right now. I have a friend in Castaic who is a handwriting expert on the side. Trustworthy and discreet. Do you feel up for a road trip today?"

"On the side? What does that mean? He's an amateur?"

Dav shook his head. "He was a professional, but retired to play in the ragtime band at Disneyland. The state still contracts with him on occasion for more difficult forgery cases."

"Wow. That's an odd mixture of skills. Hell of a commute, too."

"Do you want to come with me, or not? I need to leave in about ten minutes."

Rupe shook his head. "No. I want to stay near Hank in case he needs something. The boys can stay with me while you're gone."

"Thanks, but I'm taking them with me, and Lucas and Brittany. Rented a cabin at the lake for the afternoon so they can relax while I'm meeting with Asa nearby."

"Oh. Does Hank know you're taking them?"

"No. Probably wouldn't care, since he hasn't asked me about them even once in four days. It's really odd. Bothers me."

"He's horribly sick, Dav," Rupert answered hotly. "And he trusts you to take care of them without interfering. Don't worry about it."